TOGETHER AGAIN AT THE FOREVER HOME ON MUDDYPUDDLE LANE

Heart-warming, uplifting romance

Etti Summers

CHAPTER ONE

'*CLACTON?*' TINA SHRIEKED. 'You've never been to Clacton in your life!' She glared at her husband in disbelief.

'Somebody at the bowls club said it was nice.'

'Nice? I don't want *nice*. I want exotic! I want cocktails, white sands, turquoise sea, blue sky and sun. Not bloody Clacton!'

'Clacton's got sand and sea,' he protested.

Tina scowled at her husband. 'It hasn't got sun though, has it?'

'It has,' Neville said defensively. 'Basil from the bowls club reckons they had good weather when they went last year.'

'There's good weather in that it's not raining, and there's the type of weather where there isn't a cloud in the sky and it's warm enough to take your cardi off,' Tina retorted. 'I don't want to go anywhere where I have to pack a rain mac, thank you very much.'

Nev pulled a face. It was the same face he pulled when he didn't like something. Like when she put sprouts on his plate for instance, or somebody's car alarm went off in the middle of the night.

'We usually have good weather in June,' he argued.

They were discussing their summer holiday. Now that Tina had retired and they were able to take holidays during term time, therefore guaranteeing it would be less expensive and less busy (reasons her husband usually cited for not travelling further afield than Bournemouth), she'd been hoping to persuade him to go abroad.

She said, 'I don't want *good* weather – I want *brilliant* weather, and I don't want to wake up every morning and praying it won't rain.'

'It rains abroad,' he persisted.

Tina curbed her annoyance. 'There's less chance of it in Mexico, or Antigua, or the Seychelles.'

Nev gazed at her in disbelief and amazement. 'You want to fly all that way?'

'That's the plan,' she replied sarcastically. 'I don't think we'll be able to drive there, do you?'

The one and only time they'd been abroad, they had driven to a campsite in France: two adults, three children, and a car packed full of everything but the kitchen sink. Nev and the kids had had a great time.

Tina hadn't.

She'd spent most of the holiday scouring the local shops for something recognisable to cook that they would all like (namely things that her fussy husband would eat) and then cooking it. And although the weather had been better than the UK, it still hadn't been *lounging on the beach in a bikini with a sun umbrella casting some much-needed shade if necessary* type of weather. Not that she'd wear a bikini these days, Tina admitted to herself; at sixty-three she was a little old for it. People weren't going to want to see her saggy bits, but a nice tasteful one-piece would do the trick.

Neville's lips were pressed together and he had a frown line between his greying brows. Tentatively he suggested, 'Perhaps we could go to France again? You enjoyed it last time, didn't you?'

'No, I bloody didn't! If you think I'm going on holiday to do the shopping, the cooking, and the tidying – which is what I do at home – you need to give your head a wobble. I want to be waited on. I want a bit of luxury. I want to try different food, to experience different cultures, to do some sightseeing, and maybe go dancing in the evenings.' She wanted to go somewhere she'd never been before and do the things she'd only ever dreamt about.

She caught his confused expression and sighed. There was no point in rushing him. Hopefully she'd planted a seed; it might need a bit of watering, but if she left it for now and came back to it later, it might have begun to germinate. With Nev, things had to have time to brew. And once it had, he might give his usual *I've been thinking* speech, then suggest the very thing *she'd* suggested to *him*, but claim the idea as his own. That did grate somewhat, but as long as he came around to her way of thinking eventually, she was prepared to let it slide.

For the next half an hour they said very little, Nev sprawled in his chair watching a documentary on TV while Tina pottered around in the kitchen. Eventually he wandered out to see what she was doing, and his disappointment when he realised she wasn't preparing any food was apparent.

'What are we having for tea?' he asked.

'I was thinking perhaps we could go out,' she said. They hadn't been out in goodness knows how long; not for a proper meal. They'd been to the local pub several times for a bar snack, but that didn't count.

Nev brightened. 'It's quiz night at The Black Horse,' he said. 'I quite fancy pie and chips.'

Tina let out a snort. Pie and chips were *not* what she had in mind, and neither was a quiz. 'I was thinking we could go into Thornbury. There's a tapas place I'd like to try.'

'Tapas? Isn't that Greek?'

'Spanish, actually. Lots of little nibbles to choose from.'

'Nibbles?' he repeated doubtfully. 'That doesn't sound as though it will fill you up.'

Tina ignored the comment. 'I could wear my new dress.'

'What new dress?'

'The one I bought last month, the one you said you liked.'

He looked blankly at her, clearly having no memory of it. 'You could wear it to the pub?' he suggested hopefully.

Tina wasn't going to waste such a nice dress on a gin and tonic and pub grub. She was saving it for somewhere posher.

She tried again. 'How about that Italian place? You like Italian food.' The restaurant was a bit kitsch: there were old wine bottles with candles on the tables (very 1970s), and red and white checked tablecloths, but the food was amazing and the breadbasket was to die for.

'On our own?' Nev's tone was doubtful.

'That's the idea. Just me and you. We haven't had a romantic meal together in a long time.' Whenever they went out, it was nearly always with their friends as a foursome, or a sixsome, depending on who was available.

There was that face again, the *I don't like sprouts* face. He said, 'It's Friday. Parking in Thornbury will be dire.'

Tina rolled her eyes. Thornbury was hardly a metropolis. Admittedly it was considerably bigger than Picklewick, their little village, but it was a *rural town*. Yes, it would be busy, but it wouldn't be *crammed* with people.

'I don't think I can be bothered to drive,' he added.

'Fine, *I'll* drive.' It meant she couldn't have a drink, but to be fair, if Nev drove then neither could he.

'But you like a glass of wine with your meal,' he pointed out. 'If we go to The Black Horse, you could have two.'

As carrots went, it was a tiddler, and Tina was no donkey. Taking a saucepan out of the cupboard next to the sink, she banged it down on the hob.

Nev flinched. 'What are you doing?'

'I'm going to make some spaghetti bolognese,' she informed him crossly.

'I thought we were going to the pub?'

'You can go if you want. I'm staying here.'

'But *you're* the one who wanted to go out,' he said.

'I want to go out for a romantic meal, not to a bloody quiz night in The Black Horse.'

'You don't have to take part in the quiz. You can have a chat with the girls.'

Tina had a good circle of friends; they both did. They were other couples, around the same age, mostly with families, so they had lots in common and Tina enjoyed their company, but she wanted to do something different tonight.

These past few years (decades really), she and Nev had been stuck in a rut, constrained by the demands of work and children. Now that the kids were all grown up and the last one, Ryan, had left home, and she and Nev were both retired, she hoped they could make some time for themselves. She was painfully aware they couldn't turn back time and be the young couple they'd once been, with eyes only for each other, but they could try to recapture some of the romance, couldn't they?

The problem was that Tina saw retirement as a new chapter, as a chance to do the things that they hadn't been able to do because of said constraints; Nev, on the other hand, seemed to view retirement as the *final* chapter, the one where everything was wrapped up and wound down. Somewhere along the way he'd lost his sense of adventure and at sixty-seven had turned into an old man, content with his afternoons playing lawn bowls, his Saturday evenings in the pub, and an occasional weekday stroll along the canal with a stop off for cake and coffee along the way.

There was nothing wrong with any of that of course, but Tina wanted more. A hell of a lot more.

Her husband had that look on his face again and in one dreadful moment of utter clarity, she realised he wasn't going to change. Neville liked his life exactly the way it was.

Unfortunately, Tina *didn't.*

WHAT WAS TINA doing in the attic, Nev wondered. So far, he'd resisted the urge to go upstairs and look, in case he got roped into helping, but he could hear her bumping an object down the loft ladder and he simply couldn't resist. He had to find out what she was up to.

He was halfway up the stairs when he noticed the suitcase. Actually, not just one case, but two, were sitting on the landing, and his wife was wrestling with the loft ladder's folding mechanism.

'Here, let me do it,' he said, hurrying up the last few stairs and hastening towards her.

She didn't say anything; she simply looked at him for a second, then turned her back, picked up the suitcases and disappeared into their bedroom.

Nev wondered if she was doing what some of her friends did, and removing all her winter clothes from her chest of drawers and her side of the wardrobe in order to store them in the loft and make room for more summer outfits. He sincerely hoped not, because all those empty hangers and those sparse drawers might give her the urge to go shopping.

Anyway, it was never a good idea to put all your winter woollies in the attic when you lived in this country, since you could often have four seasons in one day. Not that the time of year made any difference to *Nev's* wardrobe (the little bit of it he had – most of it was taken up with Tina's clothes), because he tended to wear the same things all year round: trousers or jeans, tee shirts and sweatshirts, and the occasional button-down shirt when they went somewhere really nice. His only concession towards warmer days were three short-sleeved shirts and a pair of knee-length shorts. He also owned several coats, ranging from a lightweight waterproof jacket that folded up into its own little bag, through to a substantial heavy-duty winter one, but those sat happily in the wardrobe not taking up much space, and he really didn't see the point of packing them away at certain times of the year. The same went for his shoes, especially since he was no longer working and wore trainers most of the time.

More out of boredom than actual curiosity, Nev followed his wife into the bedroom. She'd unzipped both cases and placed them on the bed, and he leant against the doorframe and watched her for a moment, thinking that there didn't seem to be much sorting out going on. She appeared to be taking *everything* out of each drawer and popping them into the cases. He also noticed a holdall on the floor and a couple of those large bags she took with her when she went to the supermarket, the sturdy reusable ones that could hold a fair number of groceries.

Goodness, this didn't bode well – she was clearly planning to go on one hell of a shopping session. Neville could almost feel their bank account wincing in anticipation.

'My,' he said, 'you're having a good sort out. What's brought this on?'

Tina hesitated, then slowly turned to him. Her pretty face looked serious as she gazed at him soberly. He hoped she didn't think he was about to take umbrage that she wanted to buy herself some new outfits, because he certainly wouldn't since she rarely treated herself to anything. She'd always been the same, putting the kids, the house and him before her own needs, so it would be nice for her to go out and have a splurge. Mind you, there was nothing wrong with the clothes she already owned, but he knew what women could be like, and Tina had always dressed nicely. She took a pride in her appearance, from the top of her greying neatly bobbed hair to her dainty painted toenails.

She was still a very attractive woman, and Nev felt a sudden rush of love for her. And desire – which was unusual for a Saturday afternoon in April. He wondered what she'd do if he took her in his arms and kissed her soundly, but suspected she would probably push him away since she was in the middle of something. Anyway, her expression wasn't particularly encouraging.

'I'm leaving,' she announced.

Nev blinked. 'I'm sorry, I don't think I caught that.'

Slowly she repeated, 'I'm leaving.'

'Leaving? What do you mean, *leaving?*' She didn't normally announce that she was off out in such an odd fashion. She'd normally say, "just popping into the village", or "I'm just going to see Ryan". *Leaving* was an odd choice of word.

She dropped her gaze, and he saw her swallow hard. 'I can't do this anymore,' she said, her voice low.

'Do you want me to take over? Just show me what you want putting where, and I'll do it for you,' he offered.

'You don't get it, do you?' Her eyes shot to his, and there was a flash of annoyance in them.

'Get what?' By now, Nev was totally perplexed. What had he done wrong this time? What *hadn't* he done? Sometimes it was difficult to distinguish between the two.

Since she'd finished work a couple of months ago, she'd become ever so prickly. Maybe she was finding it difficult to adjust? She was so used to going out every day, to being busy all the time, that she might be finding it hard to adapt to a slower pace of life.

Nev hadn't found it difficult to adapt at all. He'd been more than ready to retire. He'd been so looking forward to not having to rush out of the house every morning at the crack of dawn. Or having to deal with the men on the shop floor and their never-ending grievances; worse than a bunch of kids, they'd been. He used to be a factory manager for a busy manufacturing firm and although his job should have been office based, he'd spent an inordinate amount of time out on the floor, dealing with issue after issue. He'd had his fill of it, and retirement hadn't come quickly enough.

These days, Nev relished being able to roll out of bed whenever he wanted, being able to eat a leisurely breakfast whilst watching the news, then taking a stroll into the village to pick up anything that Tina might need, or driving into Thornbury for a walk along the canal and maybe treating themselves to a little snack in one of the cafés. And twice a week he played bowls, supposedly to keep fit, but there wasn't a lot of activity involved in lawn bowls except for gentle strolling and the odd delivery of the ball. Still, he enjoyed it, more for the camaraderie and the good-natured competition than anything else.

He guessed Tina might be finding it a little more difficult, and this was manifesting itself in a desire for foreign holidays and meals out in restaurants they'd never before entertained visiting. He completely understood her wanting to be waited on, so if she brought up the subject of holidays again (which no doubt she would), he'd suggest booking into a nice hotel somewhere. Maybe not Clacton-on-Sea though, because she hadn't seemed enamoured of the idea and, truth be told, neither was he, despite the recommendation.

She'd expressed an interest in culture (who knew?) so perhaps they could go to Bath? Yes, Bath might be nice; there was plenty of culture to be had in Bath. Rather than a B&B, which was what they usually favoured, they could splash out on a nice hotel, maybe one with a spa so she could have a massage or a facial. They could even go to a bar for a cocktail, if that's what she wanted, although personally he preferred a pint in a pub. You knew what you were getting with a pint of Watneys ale.

Nev realised Tina hadn't answered his question, so he repeated, 'Get what?'

She was blinking rapidly as though she had something in her eye, and she swallowed again.

He was about to ask if she needed that looking at (excuse the pun), when she said, 'I'm leaving you, Nev. I'm leaving.'

He still wasn't sure he got it, although he had a sneaking suspicion he did as a ball of dread began to unravel in his stomach. 'You're leaving me?' he repeated. 'How? I mean, where are you going?'

'I'm going to stay at Ryan's.'

Nev was utterly bewildered. 'Ryan isn't there. He's in Germany for that convention. Anyway, he's only got a studio flat.'

'I know. It'll only be for a few days until I sort myself out and find somewhere more permanent.'

'Permanent, as in you're *not coming back*?'

'No, Nev, I'm not. I'm leaving. I'm finding somewhere else to live.' He could see the tears in her eyes as she continued, 'I can't go on like this. I want to live a little, before it's too late.'

'What do you think you're doing now?' he asked, flummoxed. 'This is living.'

'No, it isn't. This is *existing*. We're just doing the same things day in, day out, week in, week out, month in, month out. I'm sixty-three. I don't want to get to eighty-three and realise I've done nothing for the past twenty years, when I could have been enjoying myself.'

'But we *are* enjoying ourselves,' he protested, the ball of dread now turning into a lump of terror.

'*You* might be, but *I'm* not.'

'Is this about that holiday? Because if it is, we can go wherever you want. We'll go to Mexico, or the Bahamas, or...' He hunted around, trying to remember where she'd said she wanted to go, but his mind was blank.

'It's not just about the holiday. It's about what we want out of life. Your vision of retirement is totally different to mine. You're just waiting to die, when this should be a new lease of life for you – for *us*. The world is a big place, Nev, and I want to see as much of it as I can, *while* I can.'

'If that's what you want, that's what we'll do,' Nev argued desperately. 'You just say the word and we can be off tomorrow.'

'That's the problem – I *did* say the word and you weren't listening. If I stay, you might listen for a while, but you'll stop hearing, and I don't want to spend the next ten years trying to persuade you to do things you don't want to do. It's much better this way, can't you see?'

Nev couldn't. All he could see were two suitcases and an empty life without his wife. 'Don't you love me anymore? Is that it?'

Her smile was the saddest thing he'd ever seen as she said, 'Love doesn't come into it.'

'You can't leave. What about the kids?' He was clutching at straws.

'In case you hadn't noticed, they're all grown up.'

Of course he'd noticed! He'd helped pay for the deposits on their first houses, all three of them; he'd helped them move in.

That's it, he thought with sudden clarity, remembering something he'd read or heard. 'It's that empty nest thing, isn't it? What with Ryan moving out last year and you finishing work, you don't know what to do with yourself.'

'Oh, Nev.' Tina's sigh was heartfelt. 'I *do* know what to do with myself, and I'm going to do it. Now if you'll excuse me, I've got the rest of my things to pack.'

'You *can't* go.'

Wordlessly she turned her back, pulling more things off hangers and folding them into the suitcase, then she grabbed some shoes and dropped them into the empty grocery bags at her feet, as Nev stood by, wringing his hands and biting back tears, trying desperately to think of something to persuade her to stay. But she'd just told him that love didn't come into it, and what was he supposed to infer from that? That she didn't love him anymore, that's what...

Far too quickly she was done and zipping up the bulging cases. He thought he should offer to help her carry them downstairs, but he didn't want to do anything to hasten her departure or make it any easier for her to leave.

'Please don't go, Tina, I'm begging you.'

She was crying openly now. 'I have to, can't you see that?'

His heart breaking, Neville stood on the front step and watched her load her little hatchback in disbelief. This couldn't be happening. She couldn't be serious. Was she teaching him a lesson?

But he knew deep down that she *was* serious, that it *was* happening, and that she *wasn't* teaching him a lesson.

Tina, his wife of thirty-four years, was leaving him, and there wasn't a damn thing he could do about it.

CHAPTER TWO

'LIZZIE? IT'S ME, TINA. How are you?' With her mobile pressed to her ear, Tina wandered over to the window and gazed absently into the street.

The tiny one-up, one-down cottage she had found to rent in Picklewick, lacked a front garden, and sometimes when she looked out of the window she'd find herself eyeball to eyeball with a pedestrian walking by who'd happened to glance into her living room. Actually, it was a living-cum-kitchen-cum-dining room, since the downstairs living area was open plan and it was too compact to be anything else.

'Tina!' Lizzie cried. 'Lovely to hear from you! I haven't spoken to you in ages.' Her voice dropped as she asked in a much less spritely tone, 'How *are* you?'

Tina heard the subtext. Since her split from Neville, she'd been asked the same question in the same way more times than she could count.

'I'm very well, thanks. I've just come back from a holiday and wondered if you fancied a catch up?'

'A holiday? That's nice. On your own, or...?'

'On my own,' Tina confirmed firmly.

Lizzie said, 'A catch up would be great. When were you thinking of?'

'Are you doing anything today?'

'Sorry, I am. I'm busy all week, actually – got the grandchildren, you see. They're running me ragged.'

'I could do an evening?'

'Aw, I *would*, but after a day spent looking after those little monkeys, I'm not fit for man nor beast. I just want to flop in front of the TV and switch off.'

'Maybe next week, then?'

'Maybe. I'm not sure what I'll be doing yet. How about if I give you a call?'

'Okay, I—' Tina began, but before she could finish what she was going to say, Lizzie interrupted.

'I've got to go. Speak soon, Tina. Take care.'

'You too,' she said, putting the phone down on the coffee table when she realised Lizzie had ended the call and she was talking to thin air.

She sank into an armchair with a sigh. Lizzie was the second of her friends to not be available this week. Tina could understand: they had busy lives, the kind of busy life she used to have but seemed a little empty right now. She'd try one more person – Clarissa, perhaps – then she'd give up.

She'd itched to ask Lizzie how Nev was, but she hadn't dared, not wanting to put her friend in an awkward position. The problem was that all Tina's friends were Nev's friends, and vice versa. They'd been a couple for thirty-four years and had consequently developed friendships with other couples in the village. She'd known Lizzy since before she married Nev, but Lizzie's husband, Alwyn, and Nev had become firm friends over the years, and now that Tina and Nev had gone their separate ways, the split was beginning to make life a little difficult for everyone.

'I'm at a loose end this afternoon as it happens,' Clarissa told her, to Tina's surprise. 'Shall we meet in the café? Say, three o'clock? I've got a couple of errands to run first.'

'Three o'clock is perfect,' Tina agreed. *Finally*, someone she could share her holiday stories with. But when she went upstairs to pick out what to wear, Tina was fairly certain she wasn't going to tell Clarissa *everything*.

TINA WAS EARLY and Clarissa was late, so she'd ended up sitting in one of the squashy sofas near the café's window, nursing a coffee that had grown gradually cooler whilst people-watching for over forty minutes. Just as she was beginning to think her friend had stood her up, there she was, hurrying across the street. Tina waved at her through the window, and Clarissa gave her a broad smile.

Seated and with drinks orders given (Tina had a fresh coffee), Clarissa said, 'You're looking fab! Single life clearly agrees with you. How was the holiday?'

'It was great.'

'Where did you go?'

Tina could have sworn she'd told her already, but perhaps not. 'Sorrento.' She'd debated whether to go further afield, such as the Maldives, for instance, but had decided to stay closer to home for her first solo trip abroad.

'Lovely.' Clarissa sighed longingly. 'I've always wanted to go to Sorrento and the Amalfi Coast. Is it as romantic as it sounds?'

'It is,' Tina enthused. 'The scenery is so dramatic. I went to Capri, and took a trip to Naples, and went up Mount Vesuvius, and I visited Pompeii.'

'Gosh, it sounds wonderful!' Clarissa gushed. 'I'm not sure I'd want to do it on my own, though. You're for more adventurous than me.'

Tina hadn't felt adventurous at all. If truth be told, she'd felt rather flat. Make no mistake, the scenery and the sights had been jaw-dropping, but with no one to share them with, she felt they'd lacked some of the lustre they might otherwise have had. So many times she'd gone to say something to Nev, to marvel over a statue or to exclaim over a sunset, only to remember that he wasn't there. *No one* had been there. Not anyone she could relate to, at least. Yes, she'd spoken to people, but they'd been strangers, usually in pairs, or foursomes, or families. They'd been polite and had chatted, but they hadn't engaged with her in any meaningful way.

She'd been acutely aware of her solo status, and never more so than at mealtimes. The first few meals eaten at a table for one had been a novelty, or so she'd told herself. But although people watching was all well and good, she'd missed having someone to compare notes with. Besides, there was only so much people-watching she could do before feeling that everyone was people-watching *her* and wondering why she was on her own. She'd felt incredibly self-conscious most of the time. But she wasn't prepared to admit that to Clarissa.

'So, where next?' Clarissa asked, smiling at the waitress who delivered their drinks.

'Oh, I haven't decided yet,' was Tina's airy reply. 'I've only just got back.' Not only hadn't she not decided where to go, she hadn't actually decided whether she would go at all. She might long to see the sights, but seeing them on her own hadn't been as satisfying as she'd hoped. Something had been missing – and she had a horrible suspicion that the *something* was her husband.

Taking a sip of her coffee, she gathered her courage. 'Seen much of Nev?'

Their boys (men, now – but she'd always think of them as boys) had kept her abreast of what was happening, or not as the case may be, in Nev's life, but a different perspective would be welcome. Leaving him and striking out on her own hadn't flipped a switch on her feelings: she still cared about him (loved him, even), but they wanted different things. And yes, maybe it was a bit "empty nest syndrome" on her part, but this was supposed to be a new chapter in their lives, not the bloody end of it.

Clarissa's laugh was strained. 'You know Nev; same old. He doesn't change.'

And that, right there, was the problem. He'd been happy to pootle along doing the same old stuff he'd been doing for years.

Unfortunately for their marriage, Tina hadn't.

NEVILLE WAS LOOKING around the kitchen and seeing it through his youngest son's eyes. He didn't like what he saw, but didn't have the energy to do anything about it. And when did Ryan get so picky? Right up to the day the boy had moved out, his bedroom had been a complete tip. He'd rarely tidied up after himself, leaving little messes all over the house for his mother to sort out. Yet here he was, criticising Nev's housekeeping. Or lack of it, because Nev had done little in the way of cleaning since Tina had walked out over six weeks ago.

'What would Mum say?' Ryan flung out an arm, sweeping it around the kitchen. It was the only sweeping action the kitchen had seen for a while.

'She wouldn't care. She's got a new life, remember?' If Nev sounded bitter, it was because he *felt* bitter.

'She wouldn't want you—'

'Ryan, stop!' Nev pressed his lips together, imprisoning his pain behind them before continuing. 'She doesn't care.'

'But *I* do, Dad.'

Nev's eyes filled with treacherous tears. He didn't want to cry in front of his son. He didn't want his kids to worry about him, but he was clearly failing, judging by the look on Ryan's face.

'I can give you a hand, if you want,' Ryan offered.

'No, I don't want,' he snapped, instantly regretting his sharpness. Softening his tone, he added, 'I can manage.'

Ryan continued to stare at him and Nev thought he might argue, but his son let it go, saying, 'The offer is there, if you want it. Just give me a shout.'

'I will,' he promised, knowing full well that he wouldn't. This was his mess – literally, because he'd hardly done a scrap of cleaning since Tina had left – so he should be the one to sort it out.

Making a show of starting, Nev turned to the sink, grimacing at the sight of the grimy, slimy, smelly water covering the half-submerged dishes, and with his back to Ryan, he asked, 'Have you heard from your mother?'

He sensed Ryan stiffen. 'Yeah, she's okay.'

'Back safe, then?'

'Yep.'

'Good.' Nev swallowed. 'I worried about her, going all that way on her own.'

Ryan said softly, 'I know you did.'

An awkward silence followed. Nev desperately wanted more news of Tina, but it wasn't fair on Ryan to put him on the spot. But then, Ryan hadn't been fair when he'd tried to guilt Nev into cleaning up the house by bringing her into it.

'Is she happy, do you think?' he blurted, his back still turned.

A hesitation. 'She seems to be.'

'Good.' Despite his devastation and heartache, Nev was relieved. All he'd ever wanted was to make his wife happy, and if he couldn't do that anymore, then he was glad she'd managed to find happiness without him, even if his own heart was breaking because of it.

After Ryan left, Nev decided he should give the house a good clean, if only to stop his son from worrying. Ryan had his own life to lead and didn't need to be popping in every few days to check on him. Their other two lived too far away to pop in (although they were both in regular contact), so the *popping in duty* seemed to have landed on Ryan's shoulders.

Nev needed to pull himself together – but god it was hard. He missed her so much. And not just her... He missed his old life, because when she'd walked out on him, she'd taken it with her. Nothing was the same without her. Not even the bowls club, which she'd never been part of. His game was half-hearted: he went through the motions just to get out for a few hours, and the dread he felt knowing he was going back to an empty house was indescribable.

His one and only consolation was knowing that she was living her best life. He wished she'd given him a chance, though. *Another* chance, because he suspected she'd already given him plenty if only he'd realised at the time. He'd been so wrapped up in the simple joy of not having to work anymore, of being able to do what he wanted, when he wanted, that he hadn't realised they'd wanted different things out of this new stage in their lives.

He *could* have adapted; he *could* have grown to enjoy the things Tina wanted to do. But it was too late now. She'd left him, and that was that. He'd just have to get on and make the best of it.

The problem was, he didn't think he could. Life was simply too empty without her.

'RYAN! HOW LOVELY! I didn't expect to see you today!' Tina cried, standing on tiptoe to give her youngest son a kiss on the cheek, then she stood back to look at him, still unable to believe that this strapping six-foot man was her little boy. She narrowed her eyes. 'I hope you don't think I've brought you a stick of rock, because I haven't.'

'I'd prefer an actual lump of volcanic rock,' he replied, stepping into the living room and filling the small space with his presence.

'I'm fairy sure the Italians take a dim view of people nicking bits of Vesuvius,' she said, flicking the switch on the kettle. 'Tea?'

'Just a quick one.'

'Is everything alright?' Tina had a sixth sense where her boys were concerned, especially since Ryan lived in Thornbury. He wouldn't have been passing and thought he'd pop in on the off chance. 'Is it your father?'

'Relax, he's fine.'

'But you *have* been to see him? That's why you're in Picklewick, right?'

'So?' He sounded defensive.

She sighed. 'I was just asking.'

'As I said, he's fine.'

Tina wasn't convinced. She knew the boys had been checking in on him regularly – more regularly than they phoned or called in to see *her* – and she completely understood the reason for that. She was the one who'd walked out, so they naturally assumed she must be okay. And she was. It hurt a little though, that the three of them had rallied around their father more than her. Only a tad more rallying to be fair, and most people wouldn't notice, but she did.

The boys had been careful not to take sides or to lay blame, and she'd been careful not to lay blame, too. It wasn't Nev's fault they'd split up. It wasn't hers either, in a way. They'd simply grown apart, and she'd taken pains to make sure the kids understood that. It didn't matter that they were adults and that two of them had children of their own: she and Nev were still their parents, so they were bound to be affected by the break-up.

'Is he really okay?' she persisted. 'Is he eating properly—?' She broke off at Ryan's raised eyebrows. 'I still care about your father,' she added defensively. 'We were married a long time.'

'Are you going to get a divorce?'

'I don't know.' She hadn't thought that far ahead. It was the next step, she supposed, but one she wasn't ready to take just yet.

'I think you should,' Ryan said. 'It would be better all round, and especially for Dad, considering.'

What did he mean by that, she wondered. Considering... *what?* She was about to question him further when his phone pinged.

Glancing at the screen, he said, 'Damn, I've got to go. Think about it, yeah?'

And with a quick hug, he was gone, leaving her to think about nothing else for the rest of the day.

NEV TENTATIVELY pushed the door open, his stomach clenching. He hadn't ventured into their bedroom since she'd walked out on him, but it was high time he did.

The events of that day were blurred by the shock and anguish that had hit him like a wrecking ball, but he remembered flinging himself on the bed and howling like a small boy. Sometime later, he'd frantically grabbed an armful of clothes and anything else he could think of that he might need (although he hadn't really been thinking at all, just acting out of pain and instinct) and had retreated to the larger of the spare rooms. He hadn't stepped inside their marital bedroom since.

The memories instantly hit him, punching him in the gut as he surveyed the room where his world had fallen apart; the room that held so many memories of the more intimate aspects of their marriage; the room where he'd loved Tina – and lost her.

Ryan was right. He should make more of an effort. He'd been existing in a grey bubble of despair, barely summoning the energy to feed himself, going through the motions of this new life without the woman he loved.

It might be a cliché, but he was a shadow of his former self. The stuffing had been knocked out of him, and he was at a loss to know how to put a sparkle back into his world. Maybe if he did as his son urged, and had a good tidy up and a thorough clean, he might feel as though he was starting to regain control?

So that was what he did, even going as far as to don a pair of rubber gloves to tackle the frankly disgusting bathroom. He wouldn't get it all done today though, and after a couple of hours of wiping, scrubbing, washing and rinsing, he ran out of steam.

Hungry now, and thirsty, he peeled off the gloves, tossing them onto the draining board, and considered the contents of the fridge. Unsurprisingly, nothing excited him, so he put on his trainers, grabbed a jacket, and headed off to the pub. He would have a pint and something to eat there, and hopefully a bit of company. There was usually someone he could have a chat to.

Although The Black Horse had a few regulars in who he could have sat with, Nev ended up perching on a stool at the bar and chatting to the landlord between customers.

'You okay, mate?' Dave asked, swiping a cloth across the countertop with a practiced flick of his wrist.

'Can't grumble.' Nev's reply was automatic, the standard older British male's response to being asked how one was.

Dave wasn't fooled, and he raised an eyebrow in Nev's direction.

Nev took a swallow of his pint, wondering what kind of answer he could formulate. 'A bit lonely at times, that's all,' he replied eventually, hoping he wasn't being too honest. No one liked a whinger.

'I felt the same when me and my first wife split up. It'll get better, mate. Look at me – I've got Monica now, and we're as happy as pigs in clover.'

To Nev, it sounded as though Dave was advocating finding a second wife to get over the first one. But Nev couldn't imagine any other woman in his life. If he couldn't have Tina, he didn't want anyone. And he knew it was early days, but he was convinced he wouldn't change his mind.

Dave served a customer, but was back in a couple of minutes. 'It don't help right now though, does it?' the landlord empathised.

Without knowing he was going to say it, Nev blurted, 'How did you get through it?'

'Ah, now, I had my dog, didn't I? Faithful old girl, she was. She was always there for me, happy to see me no matter how much of a misery I was. And believe me, I was as miserable as sin at times.' Dave placed a serviette wrapped knife and fork on the bar next to Nev's pint. 'That's an idea – you should get yourself a dog. There's plenty to choose from at that place on Muddypuddle Lane. The Forever Home, it's called. Why don't you pick out a nice little pup to keep you company?'

Absolutely not, Nev thought. He didn't want a dog. He wanted his wife back.

But later, alone in the house, he began to wonder whether Dave might have a point. Maybe a dog *would* help? A pooch couldn't replace Tina, obviously, but it might fill a bit of the empty black hole in his heart.

CHAPTER THREE

AFTER A RESTLESS NIGHT, by seven thirty the following morning Tina had had enough, so she dragged her weary body out of bed. It was pointless fretting, going over old ground, wondering whether she'd made the right decision. Lying there with her thoughts swirling wasn't doing her any good whatsoever, so she decided she may as well begin the day.

She was looking forward to this evening, having bought a ticket to see *An Inspector Calls* in the little theatre in Thornbury. But what she was going to do between now and then, Tina had no clue.

She took her time over a breakfast of toast and marmalade, and three cups of coffee. But maybe the coffee was a mistake, because now she felt jittery and restless. Perhaps she'd walk into the village and pick up one or two bits and pieces? Not that there would be much walking involved because Picklewick was a small place and even though she lived on the outskirts it was only fifteen minutes to the high street.

It was a lovely summer morning: blue sky, the sun shining, only a few wispy clouds, flowers in full bloom, and birds chirping. She should be outside making the most of it, so perhaps a detour through the park might be nice.

Back home (she really must stop referring to the house she'd lived in for the past thirty-four years as *home*), a day like today would have seen her out in the garden, pruning, weeding, and deadheading. Unfortunately, her little rented cottage had an even littler rented garden. It was more of a yard, really. She'd bought a couple of pots and popped some annuals in them to give it some colour, but it wasn't quite the same.

She wondered how her garden was faring, and whether Nev was taking care of it. She suspected not, because the garden had mostly been her domain. He was as good as gold in doing whatever was needed doing, but she'd have to point him in the right direction and then supervise as he was doing it. Nev could not be called a green fingered chap.

She'd spent most of last night thinking about her husband, wondering if he truly was okay, wondering if he was missing her. And she hated to admit it, but *she* was missing *him*. She supposed it was only natural to miss someone who you'd spent over three decades with, and she kept on having to remind herself that being on her own was going to take some getting used to.

Somehow, she'd thought it would be a little easier than this. She'd got what she'd yearned for – the freedom to do what she wanted, when she wanted to do it – but without anyone to do it with it, that freedom had lost some of its shine.

As she entered the park gates, she told herself that new routines took time to build, and new freedoms and possibilities would also take time to assimilate. But telling herself this didn't change the reality that she was actually quite lonely. Not lonely enough to go crawling back, begging his forgiveness (that really would be a step in the wrong direction), but there was something missing from her life – and that was companionship.

She'd thought she had a good circle of friends, but they were Nev's friends as well. Maybe she needed to make some friends of her own: single friends, friends in the same boat as herself, so to speak. She was uncertain how to go about it, though. She supposed they were singles clubs in Thornbury, but she feared they were the dating kind, and she wasn't interested in dating. She was interested in friendship. She wanted someone, (preferably female, because she couldn't do with all the *does he just want to be friends or does he like me?* malarkey), who enjoyed the same things as her. Not romantic dinners, obviously, but maybe they could go to dinner or to the theatre, and in time maybe even go on holiday together.

She almost felt like she was a kid and needed her mother to invite a stranger over for a play date so she could make a new friend, and she felt quite daunted.

With nothing else to do and nowhere else to be, she decided to sit on a bench for five minutes and watch the world go by. It would be better than sitting at home watching the four walls, or the drivel on TV. At least this way she was out in the fresh air.

Tina parked her bottom, leant back, and lifted her face to the sun. The scent of mown grass hung in the air, mingling with a faint aroma of the blossom in the flowerbeds behind. The sound of children in the play area on the other side of a stand of trees reached her, and she smiled wistfully, remembering when she used to bring her own kids here to push on the swings and play on the seesaw. It seemed such a long time ago, yet it felt like only yesterday. Where had the years gone?

The warmth of the sun was making her drowsy, and she briefly closed her eyes, only to open them abruptly when something touched her leg.

'I'm so sorry,' a woman said, dragging a dog away. 'He likes going up and saying hello to people.'

Tina liked dogs and used to have one when she was growing up, but although the kids had nagged for one, she'd always refused, knowing she would be the one who would end up feeding it, walking it, grooming it, and worrying about it.

Putting out a hand for the animal to sniff, she let out a surprised giggle when its tongue flicked out and gave her a lick. 'He's very friendly,' she said.

'He really is.' The woman beamed. 'He loves everyone. You wouldn't believe the number of people I've met and talked to because of Rover. And he's great company in the house, as well. I lost my husband, you see, and I didn't know what to do with myself. I cared for him for so long – he had cancer – and I just needed something else to look after. Something else in the house. Someone to get me up in the morning. To make it worthwhile. I was dead against having a dog, but my sister fosters dogs for The Forever Home on Muddypuddle Lane and was looking after this daft thing until he could be rehomed. When I met him, that was it. It was love at first sight. I wouldn't be without him now. Right, we'd better get on. At this rate, we won't get home until teatime, as he insists on stopping and saying hello to everyone. Bye.'

Tina's gaze followed the lady and her canine companion until they were out of sight, and she let out a regretful sigh.

She'd very much enjoyed their brief chat, the simple interaction with another human being. It was the first she'd had today.

She got to her feet and carried on walking, and wasn't surprised when she rounded a corner and saw the woman chatting to another lady and her small fluffy dog.

There were other reasons why Tina hadn't given in to the children's demands for a dog over the years. She and Nev hadn't been able to agree: not on the gender, the breed, or the size. She liked larger dogs and had wanted a girl, considering she was outnumbered in a house full of males. Nev had wanted a boy dog, and a small one at that, something he wouldn't be face to face with when he was sitting on the sofa. She preferred larger dogs that she wouldn't run the risk of tripping over when she was cooking a meal or dashing upstairs with a pile of laundry in her arms.

Tina smiled as she strolled past the woman and her dog, and received a friendly smile in return, and as she walked on, the woman's voice followed. Tina glanced behind, thinking that the woman was speaking to her, then realised she was talking to her dog. Tina could have sworn the dog understood every word. The way he was looking at his mistress made her heart melt, and she envied their obvious bond.

Regretfully, she knew that a dog wasn't for her. There was no room in her life for one. She was far too busy—

Tina ground to an abrupt halt. *Too busy?* That was a joke. She had so much time on her hands now, that she didn't know what to do with it. So if she wanted, she *did* have time for a dog.

It was a thought, but one she needed to consider very carefully. After all, now that she'd made a break for freedom, did she want to encumber herself with a pet? No matter how lonely she might feel right now, it was a big commitment and not one to be rushed into. She'd mull it over, and if the idea still had legs in a few weeks, she'd revisit it.

There was no hurry; she had all the time in the world.

THE CURTAIN WENT down at the interval and Tina waited until the applause died away and most people had left their seats before she got to her feet and ambled into the foyer.

Hearing the chatter as people began comparing notes and discussing the play so far, she dearly wished she had someone to share her thoughts of the performance with. But as she was at the theatre on her own, there was no one she could talk to. Everyone else seemed to have somebody with them, either as part of a group, or as a couple; for some reason she seemed to be the only lone person. She knew it was ridiculous, because there would be other people here on their own too, but she feared she stuck out like a sore thumb. Every so often somebody's gaze would alight on her and then slide away, as though her solitary status might be catching. She knew that was daft, but she couldn't help how she felt.

The queue for the ladies' loo offered some relief in more ways than one, since most of the women standing in line were on their own. Totally out of character for her and contrary to what she would normally do,

Tina half turned and said to the woman behind, 'What do you think of it so far?'

'I've always loved this play,' the woman said. 'I think I must have seen it four or five times now. The last time was in London. We made a weekend of it. When I heard it was coming to Thornbury, I said to my husband that we simply had to go and see it, and he rolled his eyes. Bless him, he did agree to come with me, but I think he's so bored he dropped off at one point. I hope none of the actors noticed!'

Tina said, 'I studied it at school, but that was many years ago now and I've forgotten quite a bit, so it feels like a completely new experience for me.'

'Oh, I wish I could see it again for the first time!' the woman cried, then she jerked her head and pointed. 'There's a cubicle free.'

So there was.

After Tina left the ladies' loos, she headed towards the bar, then halted and stared in dismay. It was crammed so full of people that she had a feeling the curtain would go up again before the last person was served.

Did she want to wait?

Not really.

Wishing she'd brought some water with her, she returned to the auditorium and there she sat, waiting for people to slowly trickle back in to retake their seats.

Having read the programme from cover to cover three times, she didn't want to read it again, so she people watched for a few minutes, then felt so self-conscious that she took out her phone. She'd switched it to aeroplane mode, not wanting to be that person whose phone rang in the middle of a performance, but she needn't have worried – she had no missed calls, no messages, and no notifications.

There wasn't even anyone she felt she *could* message to say, 'Guess where I am?' and proceed to tell them how much she was enjoying herself. Because... she wasn't.

If she was honest, she was having a bit of a miserable time. She thought about the man who'd seen this play so many times he was bored stiff and falling asleep, and she snorted. That would be Nev. He'd be falling asleep and bored rigid, but not because he'd seen it so many times, but because this wasn't his kind of thing. She wasn't even sure whether he would have accompanied her if she'd asked. He probably would have complained about the parking and used that as an excuse not to come.

Tina wasn't sure what made her do it, but by the time the second half of the play was about to start, she'd managed to find herself on Picklewick's dog rehoming site. And she was so engrossed in looking at all those sweet faces with their pleading eyes and cute expressions, that the woman seated next to her had to ask her to put her phone away.

Abashed, Tina hastily turned it off, slipped her mobile into her bag, and tried to concentrate on the stage in front of her and on the story unfolding. But one of those little faces had struck a chord, and she simply had to take another look.

She wasn't enjoying herself anyway, so with a great deal of embarrassment and many whispered apologies, she made her way to the end of the row and hurried out of the theatre, her face flaming. Once in the foyer, she told herself she'd never meet any of those people again, and so what if they'd tutted at her? She was just glad to be out of there.

Before she made her way back to the car (she noted that *she'd* had no trouble parking) she turned her phone on again, and the page she'd been looking at sprang into life.

Tina gazed at the image on the screen. The face staring back at her had bright brown eyes and a lolling pink tongue. It belonged to a dog called Daphne, and according to the description underneath, she was a black and white greyhound, approximately three to four years old and in need of a calm, quiet, loving home due to her anxious nature.

Tina could certainly provide the calm and quiet, and the way she was feeling right

now, she was more in need of love than
the dog.

Perhaps it wasn't such a bad idea? She'd
have some company, someone to talk to,
although they wouldn't answer back
(actually, that might be a good thing). The
dog would always be pleased to see her,
and Tina would have someone to care for,
someone to give her a reason to get up in
the morning. And as for going on holiday
and all the other things she'd planned on
doing – which hadn't worked out too well
for her up to now, but she lived in hope –
there were always dog sitters who she'd
be able to leave her with.

'Tina and Daphne...' She said the names
aloud, liking the feel of them in her mouth.
They could be a duo, like Thelma and
Louise, minus the dubious ending.

As Tina drove home, the more she thought about it, the more the idea appealed. But she didn't want any old dog. She wanted *Daphne.*

When she went to bed later that night, she promised herself she'd give The Forever Home a ring in the morning, and as she drifted off to sleep, she found she was very much looking forward to meeting her new companion.

CHAPTER FOUR

THE FOREVER HOME was located at the top of Muddypuddle Lane, which lay on the outskirts of Picklewick. The lane itself was narrow and steep, leading up from the main road, past a riding stable and then a farm, before becoming more of a dirt track as it continued upwards to the top of the mountain. The view out over the valley was gorgeous, but Tina's mind was on other things and she didn't pay it a great deal of attention.

The Forever Home was actually a boarding kennel, but it also housed dogs from the animal sanctuary in Thornbury – a kind of satellite outpost – and this was where Daphne was being housed. Telling herself she needed to keep an open mind when it came to whatever dog she was going to adopt, although she'd set her heart on the greyhound, Tina pulled onto a gravelled parking area and cut the engine. When she got out of the car, she could hear the voices of numerous dogs. No wonder the kennels were situated in such an out of the way place, she thought wryly.

A sign pointed the way to reception, and she headed in that direction. Apparently, every afternoon between two o'clock and four, The Forever Home was open for call-in sessions, so although she didn't have an appointment, she was hoping to be able to see Daphne today.

It occurred to her that maybe she should have rung first, but she was here now so she might as well go in and ask.

A young woman with long blonde hair tied back in a ponytail sat behind the desk and looked up with a smile as Tina entered. 'Good afternoon,' she said. 'It's a lovely day, isn't it? What can I do for you?'

Overcome with unexpected nerves, Tina replied, 'I'm here about a dog.'

'Do you want to board one, or are you here about the rescue dogs?'

'A rescue dog.'

'Okay, in that case, let me find someone to help you. Jakob is on duty today, so I'll just give him a shout.'

Jakob turned out to be a big man with a gruff voice and kind eyes. When Tina told him she was looking to adopt and that Daphne had caught her eye, his face broke into a smile.

'She's a very sweet girl,' he said. 'A little on the anxious side, but then this is a strange situation for most dogs, so it's to be expected.'

'Can I meet her?'

'Certainly. Follow me.'

Tina gazed around curiously as Jakob led her through the kennel block and showed her into an area reminiscent of a barn. It contained a wooden benched seating area, a dirt floor covered in straw, a box of dog toys, and a large water bowl.

'This is our meet-and-greet pen,' he explained. 'Take a seat and I'll go fetch her for you.'

Instinctively, Tina knew that once she set eyes on the dog, there would probably be no going back. If she had any doubts, now was the time to make her apologies and leave. But she didn't. Instead, she sat there, her hands clasped in her lap, and waited as patiently as she could.

The wait seemed interminable but was probably only a few minutes, and when she heard footsteps approaching, accompanied by the click of claws on concrete, she sat up straight, feeling unaccountably nervous.

With her heart in her mouth, she watched the door open, and her gaze latched onto the graceful white and black hound as it cautiously stepped inside.

Tina was instantly smitten. The dog's ears and tail were down, and her gentle face looked worried. In the delicate prancing way that greyhounds have, she picked her way across the pen, her eyes locked onto Tina's.

'Hello, sweetheart,' Tina croon softly, holding out a hand for the dog to sniff.

Daphne's tail wagged uncertainly, and she licked her lips.

Jason interpreted for her. 'As you can see, she's a little anxious, but she'll soon thaw out when she gets to know you.' He unclipped her lead from the harness.

Daphne didn't move.

'What's her background?' Tina asked.

'She came in as a stray, so we honestly don't know. We think she's between three and four years old, hasn't had puppies, so we don't think she's been used for breeding, and she's been spayed. She's used to being handled, is friendly, and she doesn't appear to have been ill-treated in any way. She's in good health and doesn't have any behavioural issues, apart from the anxiety. But we're working on that, aren't we, girl? Are you happy for me to leave you alone to get acquainted, or would you like me to stay for a bit?'

'You can go. I'm sure Daphne and I will soon become firm friends.'

Tina knew better than to rush things, so she sat quietly, just watching as the dog cautiously sniffed around the pen. Tina guessed Daphne was using it as a delaying tactic until she felt more comfortable with this strange human.

'Would you like to come home with me, sweetheart? You'll have your own comfy bed, lots of cuddles, and I'll take you for a walk every single day, I promise.'

Daphne glanced in her direction and her tail wagged again.

'You'd like that, would you? And we can go to the pet shop and you can choose your own toys, and there'll be plenty of treats, but not too many.'

More tail wagging was followed by Daphne gradually moving closer until she was standing right next to Tina.

Tina put out her hand again and gently stroked the dog's silky ears. She was so soft, and when Tina looked into those liquid brown eyes, her heart melted into a puddle.

It was a good half an hour before Jakob came back to check on them, and when he did, it was to find Tina and Daphne sitting on the floor together, the dog with her head resting in Tina's lap, and Tina singing to her.

Not in the least self-conscious, Tina beamed up at him. 'She's perfect. Please can I have her?'

Jakob had an answering smile on his face. 'There are a few formalities to go through first, and you'll need a home visit.

Assuming that goes okay, I can't see why not.'

Reluctantly Tina got to her feet, Daphne by her side, and she laid a protective hand on the dog's head, not wanting to leave her. It was going to be a wrench going home without her, but it couldn't be helped. And the delay would give her time to get the house ready for the dog's arrival.

As Tina drove home, her heart was full and she was brimming with excitement for this brand-new chapter in her life. She and Daphne were going to be a team, and she couldn't wait to get the dog home.

But underneath the anticipation lay a more sombre feeling that she was trying her best to ignore. A feeling that although the dog might give her some of the love and companionship lacking in her life,

Daphne was no substitute for the love and companionship of the man she'd walked out on.

WHY COULDN'T PEOPLE be happy for her, Tina asked herself. Why did they have to rain on her parade? She'd bumped into Clarissa in the village on the way to the pet shop, and when she'd informed her friend that she was adopting a rescue dog, she'd received a less than enthusiastic response.

'Why would you want to adopt a dog?' Clarissa asked. 'You've been telling everyone you want to travel, yet you want to tie yourself down with a pet?'

'I don't consider it "tying myself down",' Tina retorted, disgruntled.

'But I thought you wanted to do things, like go on holidays and do the stuff that Nev didn't want to do? You can't just hop on a plane if you've got a dog to think about. You've got to find a kennel, and that costs money. And what if you want to go out for the day? You can't leave it on its own for any length of time, can you?'

'I'll work something out,' Tina retorted, not wanting to admit that going on holiday alone wasn't all it was cracked up to be. And neither were days out. Wandering around a stately home wasn't going to be much fun on her own, she'd realised. She would go out for long walks instead, with Daphne by her side. And she was also secretly hoping that Daphne would help her make friends. People spoke to dogs, didn't they? Dog walkers seem to be a friendly bunch. Maybe she could join a rambling club and meet people that way?

'Well, I'm sure you know best,' Clarissa sniffed, her tone indicating that she honestly didn't think Tina knew best at all.

And maybe Tina didn't. She'd made a complete hash of things so far, so she clearly didn't have a clue. Now and again, in the long hours of the night, she asked herself whether she'd done the right thing in leaving Nev, or whether she should have just accepted her life as it was, boring and uneventful, but at least she'd had somebody to talk to. Although she'd felt stifled and hemmed in at the time, was this any better?

Clarissa said, 'I can't wait until Fred and I retire. We're going to have a high old time, and we're going to do our best to spend the kids' inheritance. Fred's talking about buying a camper van and touring Europe, and although it *sounds* romantic, I think the reality will be very different. I'd prefer to rent a villa for three months and spend the winter in the sun. You could do something like that, couldn't you?' She paused dramatically, then added, 'Oh no, you won't be able to, not if you've got a dog.'

To Tina, renting a villa sounded lovely, except for one small detail – she would *still* be on her own, but with the unwelcome addition of prickly heat and the risk of sunburn.

There was only one thing that Tina took away from the conversation, and that was the idea of touring in a campervan.

Now *that* would be an adventure!

NEV'S GUT TWISTED and an abrupt pain stabbed him in the heart as he drove along Picklewick's high street and caught sight of his wife chatting with Clarissa. Hastily he dragged his eyes away and focused on the road ahead, not wanting to cause an accident, but his mouth was dry and his eyes blurred with unexpected tears.

This wasn't the first time he'd seen Tina since they'd split up, and each time it was like a knife to his heart. From the brief glimpse he'd got, she looked well, he thought. And happy.

He glanced in the rear-view mirror and saw her wave cheerily to Clarissa and trot off down the road with a bounce in her step. He wanted to pull over and go running after her, and beg her to come back, but he didn't. Instead, he stared straight ahead and concentrated on his driving.

He was on his way to the animal sanctuary at the top of Muddypuddle Lane, in the hope he might find a companion – something to love him the way his wife used to – and clearly didn't any longer. He wasn't convinced he would adopt a dog at this stage, but he was keeping an open mind.

Looking for a connection of some kind, such as love at first sight, was unrealistic, he knew. He wouldn't simply just fall in love with a dog. Not the way he'd fallen in love with Tina the first time he'd set eyes on her. He remembered it as though it were yesterday; but before he could let his mind wander down that particular road, he was trundling up Muddypuddle Lane, the car's engine labouring as it navigated the potholed gradient.

Having lived in Picklewick all his life, Nev knew the area well, and he recalled playing up here when he was a boy, building dens in the ferns, damming small tumbling streams, and lying in the heather listening to the skylarks and feeling the sun on his face.

The Forever Home had been built on a site of an old derelict farmhouse on the top of the gently rolling mountain. The current owners had restored it, doing a beautiful job – from the outside at least, he noted – and several other buildings had sprung up next to it.

He could hear the dogs long before he saw them, and as he made his way to the reception area, he winced. He didn't think he could live with that kind of racket, day in, day out, and he didn't envy the owners, but each to his own, he supposed. The Forever Home had originally been set up

,as a boarding kennel, but the sanctuary in Thornbury needed some additional facilities and was now housing a selection of the dogs in their care here.

The kennels themselves were owned by a young woman called Maisie, along with her partner Adam, but the guy who was responsible for the rehoming side of things was called Jakob, and it was Jakob who Nev was speaking to now.

'I'm only *thinking* about getting a dog,' Nev warned, after the man had explained the adoption process to him. 'I haven't totally decided yet.'

'That's fine,' Jakob replied. 'It's a big decision. Why don't you come back when you're ready?'

'Do you think I could take a look around now? See if anything catches my eye?'

'This isn't like a car showroom. A dog is a living, breathing creature with feelings.' Jakob's tone was sharp.

'I know that, but it has to feel right, you know?'

The man's tension eased. 'I know, that's why you need to seriously think whether this is what you want.' He drew in a breath, then relented. 'I can get a few details if you like, and if I think there's a dog that might be suitable, I'll set up a meeting and we'll take it from there.'

'Fair enough, but I don't want anything too big,' Nev warned.

Jakob nodded. 'We've got all sizes here, and all kinds of breeds,' he said, and after he'd asked Nev a series of questions, he led him towards the block of kennels.

The barking got louder as they approached the building, and Nev bit his lip. The house was far too quiet, *painfully* quiet, without Tina, but he didn't want to fill it with a barking dog.

'They're noisy, aren't they?' he said.

Jakob shot him a look. '*You'd* probably be yelling a bit if you were shut up in a cage,' he retorted.

Nev let out a laugh. 'Sorry, yes, you're probably right. I wouldn't be happy.'

The man said, 'I prefer a barking dog to a shutdown dog. The barky ones are ready to get out of this place and find their forever homes. The shutdown ones have given up. They're the most pitiful.' He came to a halt outside a door and pushed it open. 'This is our meet-and-greet area. You wait here and I'll go find you a dog I think might be a good match for you. I'll be back in a minute.'

Nev took a seat on a wooden bench and gazed around the barn-like interior, his knee jiggling. Was this moving too fast? He'd only wanted to make inquiries, and now he was waiting to see a dog. Mind you, it was his own fault; he didn't *have* to look around. And neither did he have to take the first one they offered. He could hold out for something else, he thought. Then he recalled what Jakob had said about this not being a car showroom, and he felt ashamed. This wasn't a shopping expedition – this was more like a first date. No wonder he felt nervous.

Jakob quickly returned with a bundle of tan and white energy on the end of a lead. The dog was a smooth-coated terrier with bright black eyes, short stumpy legs, and a small but sturdy body. The animal's ears were pricked, his tail was up, and he oozed confidence.

'Meet Peanut,' Jakob said, and unclipped the dog's lead. 'He's a Jack Russell terrier.'

Peanut immediately bounced over to Nev and without warning launched himself into Nev's lap.

'Crikey!' Nev exclaimed. 'He's keen, isn't he?' The dog tried to lick his face and Nev had to fend him off with one arm.

Jakob laughed. 'I think it's safe to say he likes you.'

Nev felt quite flattered. The dog's unbridled enthusiasm was the most affection he'd had in a while.

'He's a bit of a pocket-rocket but he'll calm down in a minute,' Jakob assured him. 'He can be excitable and this is a new situation for him.'

'At least I know he's friendly,' Nev pointed out.

'He's that alright; he loves everyone.'

'Why is he here? Couldn't his owners cope with him?' Nev was wondering whether *he* could, considering the dog's abundant energy.

'He's a stray, so we don't know what happened to him, unfortunately. Hopefully nothing bad, but you can't really tell. He was found by the canal in Thornbury. A member of the public brought him in. It's an altogether too familiar scenario, I'm afraid. We don't know whether he got out, or whether he was abandoned. Either way, the owner couldn't be traced, so he came to us.'

Peanut, who had been trying to lick Nev's face off, had calmed down considerably and was now nudging his hand, asking to be petted. Nev duly obliged. He was a sweet little thing, he thought, as the dog rolled over onto his back to show his tummy. Nev scratched the dog's soft underbelly and Peanut let out little whimpers of happiness.

'He certainly likes being fussed,' he observed.

'He'll put up with any amount of attention. If you were up for it, he'd let you do that all day.'

'So he's not just a little pocket rocket,' Nev said. 'That's good to know. I want a dog who will cuddle with me on the sofa.'

'As you can see, he enjoys a cuddle fest. But he's also got a lot of energy for a small dog, so will need to be walked every day.'

'I'm up for that.' It would get him out of the house and give *him* some much-needed exercise, as well as the dog. 'I've told you I'm retired,' Nev said, 'but I don't expect to be at home all day, every day. Will it be okay to leave him for a couple of hours if I want to go to the pub, say?'

'I don't see why not. Some dogs are happier in their own company than others, and some have separation anxiety, but I don't believe Peanut is one of them. He's far too confident and cocky for that. If anything, he can be a bit on the independent side, like most terriers.'

'What do you say, Peanut?' Nev stared at the dog. The dog stared back at him and Nev was sucked into his gaze. Was he imagining it or were those eyes begging him to take him home?

Jakob stepped forward, the lead in his hand. 'Right then, let's put you back in your pen,' he said to the dog. 'It's four o'clock, so I'm going to have to kick you out, I'm afraid.' This last was said to Nev.

Nev didn't want to go. He wanted to stay here with his new friend.

The realisation was a telling one.

And in that moment, Nev understood that sooner or later this dog would be going home with him.

CHAPTER FIVE

TINA WATCHED DAPHNE cautiously sniff her way from one end of the room to the other. Her living-cum-dining-cum-kitchen was tiny and it shouldn't have taken the dog long, but she seemed to spend ages sniffing and ignoring Tina. Tina felt a little hurt, but realised that this whole situation was entirely new for Daphne; the poor pooch had no idea where she was or what she was doing here. Tina wished she could explain it to her, but since that was impossible, the only thing she could do was let Daphne get on with it.

It was mid-morning, so she decided to make a cup of coffee and go sit in the small yard to drink it. She'd take a biscuit, just the one, and see if she could tempt

Daphne into taking a morsel of it from her. Greyhounds were naturally slim, but this dog appeared to be skinnier than normal. Jakob had explained that she wasn't an enthusiastic eater, and sometimes he had to tempt her. He did say that some dogs didn't settle well into kennel life, and Daphne had been one of them. He advised Tina to give her time to get used to her and her new surroundings, and gradually she'd become the dog she was meant to be.

Leaving the door open, Tina sat outside, and as she sipped her coffee, she kept an eye on Daphne. The dog had paused in the middle of the kitchen area and was peering out at her. Tina looked away, picked up the biscuit, and took a small nibble.

Delicately, one paw at a time, Daphne ventured outside, where she began the sniffing ritual all over again. Similar to the inside, the outside of the cottage was small and the dog soon completed her first circuit, then went round for a second time, and a third. Tina pretended to ignore her, and the more she did, the more she became aware of the dog shooting her furtive, anxious glances.

Daphne's ears pricked up as Tina had another nibble of the biscuit, and when she pointedly placed the remainder back on the table, the dog's gaze followed.

'Would you like some?' she asked.

Daphne returned to her sniffing, but Tina noticed her edging closer.

Eventually the dog arrived at the table and she gently placed the end of her muzzle on one corner.

'Ah, so you *would* like some! There's a good girl.' Tina picked up what was left of the biscuit and held it out.

Daphne sniffed it cautiously before very delicately taking it out of Tina's hand. There was a bit of a crunch, then it was gone, and the dog was licking her lips.

'You're not having anymore,' Tina told her. 'Human food isn't good for you. But if you're hungry, I've got some special dog treats.'

Some was an understatement. Tina had stocked up on virtually everything the pet shop had that was dog-related. The guy who ran it must have thought all his Christmases had come at once, because Tina had spent a fortune. She'd also been given a blanket from Daphne's kennel at The Forever Home, and some of the food they'd fed her there. The first was to provide some familiar comfort, and the second was to keep her digestion on an even keel. It was mostly dried kibble, and Tina didn't think it looked at all appetising. But Jakob was the expert, so who was she to argue? However, it hadn't stopped her from buying a selection of differing foods and treats. Over the course of the next few weeks she'd try them out on Daphne and see which ones she preferred. Anyway, it must be boring eating the same old food all the time, and Tina would hate being served the same meal every evening, so maybe Daphne's lack of appetite was due to boredom.

Jakob had also suggested that Tina should carry on with her day as normal, and let Daphne slot in with her routine. She was a bright girl and would soon pick up on what was expected of her, but just ensure she had enough attention and exercise.

Thinking that Daphne had had enough excitement for a couple of hours, Tina decided to make some lunch, then settle down and read a book for an hour or so before taking her for a walk. Hopefully Daphne would also settle down and stop pacing around, and Tina was keeping her fingers crossed that the dog would actually come in for a snuggle at some point. Maybe not today, though. She was realistic enough to realise it could take a while for Daphne to learn to trust her and for their bond to develop. On Tina's part, she was already in love with the sweet natured dog, and she was finding it comforting having another presence in the house. She didn't feel as alone and as she prepared a light lunch, she found herself telling Daphne what she was doing as though the dog were one of her grandchildren and she was explaining to them how to make a sandwich.

'I prefer seeded bread,' she told Daphne, who was sitting in the middle of the living room staring at her. 'It's tastier and it's more filling, and I think it's probably better for you. Not that *you're* going to get any, of course, because bread isn't good for dogs. Neither is ham really – it's probably too salty – but you can have a little bit.'

She placed a morsel on one side of the plate ready to give to the dog, then set about rinsing some lettuce, a couple of tomatoes and a chunk of cucumber. With the salad ingredients suitably washed and dried, she arranged them on the bread, placed two slices of ham on top and added a generous dollop of mayonnaise.

'There,' she said, 'sandwich all done.'

She sat at the little table to eat it. Daphne stayed where she was, but she didn't take her eyes off Tina's lunch, watching every single movement of the sandwich as it was gradually consumed. Before she took the last bite, Tina offered Daphne the spare ham.

Daphne got to her feet and came warily towards her.

Tina said, 'It's just a nice bit of ham. Nothing nasty, I promise. You'll like it.'

Once again Daphne sniffed it, then took it from her very gently and it was gone in one gulp.

'I'll quickly wash up, then we'll go for a walk. You'll like that, won't you?' Tina was going to go to the park for their first excursion. They wouldn't go far this afternoon, but tomorrow she'd take her a little further.

Tina had bought Daphne three harnesses in differing colours, with matching leads.

She'd also debated buying her a coat, but considering it was the height of summer, she thought perhaps it was overkill. Although, thinking about it, she should have got her a lightweight waterproof one for wetter outings. She'd remedy that tomorrow, she decided. Their morning walk could be around the park, and then they could take a little detour into the village and pop to the pet shop, where she'd try to limit herself to just buying the waterproof coat.

Daphne stood tense and wary as Tina put her harness on her, but as soon as the lead was clipped to it and they headed out the door, the dog had a bounce in her step.

'You like going for walks? I'm sure you're going to love the park. There are lots of other dogs, and there'll be loads of things to sniff, because that's what you are, a sniffer.' The dog gave her a quick glance, and Tina stroked her smooth head.

The park wasn't large but it was pretty, with a children's play area, paved pathways, flowerbeds, trees, and a nice open field in the centre. As soon as they entered through the wrought-iron gate, Tina immediately spotted another dog walker, and a mad springer spaniel with an ever-wagging tail was hightailing it after a ball, grabbing it as it bounced. The dog snatched it out of the air and dashed back to its owner to drop the ball at the man's feet, then bark. The man threw it again and the dog shot after it joyfully.

Daphne had stiffened when she'd spotted the other dog, but quickly relaxed, and then didn't seem to take any more notice of it. She wasn't even interested in the ball. She did, however, give a little wag of her tail when the spaniel's owner said hello to her, before he greeted Tina.

When he saw her bemused expression, he explained, 'I always speak to the dog first, and then the owner. She's a lovely girl. What's she called?'

'Daphne,' Tina told him.

On hearing her name, the dog's ears pricked up and she gave another little wag.

He said, 'I love greyhounds. They're so gentle. Not like Sparky.' The spaniel had brought the ball back again for his owner to throw, which he duly did. 'He can keep this up for hours. Absolutely bonkers, he is, but I wouldn't swap him for the world.'

For some reason Tina felt compelled to say, 'I only got Daphne today. She's a rescue.'

'*Today?* Good on you. Sparky's a rescue, too. We've had him since he was a year old because his previous owners couldn't cope. He was too lively for them. You wouldn't believe he's eight, would you?'

'Gosh, no, I wouldn't.'

'How old is Daphne?'

'Three or four, they think. She was a stray, so the shelter didn't know much about her.'

'Good luck – not that you'll need it. We'll probably see you again. We're in the park most days.'

Tina was smiling to herself as she walked off, Daphne trotting by her side, and it didn't surprise her when a woman with a Labrador said hello. Dog walkers seemed quite a friendly bunch, she thought, as she said hello back.

By the time she returned home she'd met three dog walkers and four dogs, because one person had two small chihuahuas who'd been rather vocal. The dogs that is, not their owner. Although, their owner had stopped to say hello, and she'd also apologised, saying that the dogs were all bark and no bite, but they liked to make their presence known.

Daphne had shown great interest in them when she'd spotted them from some distance away, but the closer they'd got the more her interest had waned, until it had disappeared altogether when they'd drawn level, when she'd only given them a cursory glance before ignoring them.

'That was nice,' Tina said as she removed Daphne's harness and tickled her ears. Daphne wagged her tail. Just a little wag, nothing enthusiastic, but it was a start, and as Tina cooked her evening meal,

Daphne took up position by the fridge, watching the goings on with interest.

'Do you like the smell of lasagna? You can't have any, but I've got a yummy pouch of lamb and winter vegetables you can have instead,' she told the dog. Daphne studied her movements intently, her nose constantly twitching due to the enticing smells coming from the oven.

When Tina sat down to eat, she placed Daphne's bowl on the floor next to her.

Daphne ignored it. She didn't even bother to check out what was in it. Instead, she let out a sigh and went to lie by the front door.

'What's wrong with your nice comfy bed?' Tina asked.

Daphne rested her muzzle on her nose and stared into the distance.

'Are you tired? Is that it? It's been an exciting day for you, hasn't it?'

As a conversationalist, Daphne left a lot to be desired, and although Tina knew the dog wasn't going to answer her, she had hoped for a bit more of a reaction. Still, as she kept telling herself, it was early days. This was day one of their new life together, and it was going to be a period of adjustment for both of them.

By the time Tina settled down on the sofa that evening to watch TV, Daphne had moved from her position by the front door and was now curled in a ball by her feet. Tina stared down at her. The dog was all legs, paws and tail, her nose buried in her flank, her eyes tightly closed.

When Tina leant forward to pat her, she jerked awake. Her head came up and she looked momentarily confused, probably wondering where she was. Then she must have remembered, because she sighed again and dropped her head.

Tina sensed there'd be a while to go before Daphne accepted her, but she didn't mind. After all, she had all the time in the world.

Abruptly it struck her that the reason she had all the time in the world was because she didn't have anything else to do, and a wave of intense loneliness and regret swept over her.

What had she done? She and Nev had been bimbling along together just fine, but she'd thrown it all away for the lure of a more exciting life.

And now Ryan had hinted that his father wanted a divorce.

Tina let out a little moan and Daphne uncoiled herself and sat up. With her brown eyes looking deep into Tina's, the dog rested her chin on Tina's knee, and Tina stroked her head. Feeling very sorry for herself and fearful that she'd made the biggest mistake of her life, Tina was in desperate need of comfort, and despite vowing not to allow the dog on the furniture, she patted the empty space on the sofa next to her and Daphne obediently clambered onto it and cuddled into her.

'I've made my bed, Daphne, and I have to lie in it. Let's face it, I'm not going to be flitting off all over the world on my own. I'm simply not built for it. Maybe it would be different if I could take you with me, then at least I'd have some company. I'll just have to be content with holidays in this country. I'm sure there are dog friendly cottages and apartments out there if I fancy a break by the seaside.'

Then she remembered Clarissa mentioning a camper van, and though maybe it wasn't such a bad idea after all?

CHAPTER SIX

'WHAT'S THAT NOISE?' Ryan asked.

Nev thought it was obvious. 'It's a dog,' he replied, raising his voice to be heard over the racket. He had his mobile phone pressed to one ear and a finger jammed in the other, trying to block out the noise, because he was having difficulty hearing his son over Peanut's barking.

'Where are you, Dad?'

'In the house.'

'It sounds like the dog is in the room with you,' Ryan joked.

'That's because he is.'

'Why would you have a dog in your house?'

Unable to hear himself think, Nev took the mobile away from his ear and dropped his hand to his side as he yelled, 'Pipe down, Peanut!' Then he put the phone back to his ear. 'Sorry about that.'

'Did you say something about peanuts?'

'No, that's the dog's name. I was telling him to be quiet.'

'But why is he in your house?' Ryan asked again.

'Because he's *my* dog.'

Ryan's response was lost in a flurry of barks.

Losing patience, Nev said, 'Hang on.' He put the phone down, picked up the dog, took him outside and deposited him in the garden, shutting the door firmly. The immediate reduction in noise level was a blessed relief. God only knows what had set him off this time.

Resuming the call, Nev said, 'That's better. Shall we start again?'

'Why have you got a dog?'

'For company. I was rattling around in this house on my own. It was too quiet, too empty.' His laugh had a manic quality as he added, 'It certainly isn't quiet now.'

Peanut was a barker. He barked at lots of things, but what really got him going was other dogs. Nev wasn't sure whether the terrier wanted to say hello to them or squabble with them. He hadn't dared let him get close enough to another mutt to find out. And the bigger the dog, the more desperate Peanut was to get to it. The only redeeming feature was that every time this happened, Peanut's tail was wagging. Thank goodness he was only a small dog, so it was easy enough to drag him away; or failing that, Nev could scoop him up. He hadn't had to do it yet, but he knew there might come a time.

At least Nev wasn't bored now. How could he be, when the little mutt was taking all his time and attention? He'd only had him three days but he hadn't had five minutes to himself. If Peanut wasn't asking to go out, he was asking to be played with, or to have a belly rub, or was begging for food. No wonder the guy at The Forever Home had called him a pocket rocket. The little bugger didn't know what it was to sit still.

'What on earth is up with you and Mum?' Ryan asked. 'She's gone and got herself a dog, as well.'

Nev was taken aback. 'She *has?* When?'

'I don't know – about a week ago?'

'What sort of dog? '

'A greyhound.'

'I thought you said her house was tiny. Those cottages on Blossom Lane are barely big enough to swing a cat.'

'I know.'

'Why has she got a dog?'

'I've no idea.'

'That's going to cramp her style. She won't find it as easy to take off for foreign climes at the drop of a hat when she's got a dog to consider,' Nev observed.

'I've told her that, but she didn't seem to care. Between you and me, I get the feeling she doesn't think going abroad is all it's cracked up to be.'

Nev shook his head in disbelief. His wife of thirty-four years had claimed she was leaving him because she wanted trips around the world, wanted to eat in romantic restaurants, and go dancing. Clearly she'd been lying. It might have been to spare his feelings, but if that was the case, it hadn't worked. He wished she'd just told him she'd fallen out of love with him and be done with it. But that still didn't answer the question of why she'd got herself a dog when she'd resisted any attempts by the boys to persuade her to have one in the past.

After he said goodbye to his son, he let the still barking Peanut back in.

'All right, boy, that's enough,' he muttered as Peanut launched himself into Nev's arms and began trying to lick his face, his tail going nineteen to the dozen. He clearly hadn't appreciated being shoved outside into the garden.

Maybe Tina felt vulnerable living on her own, so that's why she got such a big dog,

Nev mused, wondering if it was as lively as Peanut, because no one would dare break in with this one making a racket.

'What do you think, Peanut? Do you think Tina's got a dog because she doesn't like being in a house on her own?'

Peanut squirmed and wriggled in Nev's arms, and he put him down.

'I suppose I'd better take you out for a walk,' he said grimly, not looking forward to it. He was beginning to wonder whether adopting Peanut was a mistake. The dog was simply too shouty.

Nev wouldn't give up on him just yet, though. Jakob had warned there might be teething problems, and the dog would need time to settle into his new environment. Nev would also need time to get used to having a dog around the place, and it occurred to him that Peanut might be picking up on Nev's own anxiety. He'd heard that dogs could be very intuitive, so maybe Peanut was responding to that. Nev vowed to try to relax a little and not get so het up. Maybe he could look into doing a bit of training with him?

On impulse, he went to the fridge and took out some chicken. He'd bought a precooked bird from the supermarket yesterday as he couldn't be bothered to cook for himself, and there was plenty leftover. He knew Peanut liked chicken because he'd fed him a portion for his tea last night, along with a handful of those biscuits The Forever Home had supplied him with. To Nev's eyes they didn't look particularly appetising, even though he'd been assured they contained everything a dog needed, dietary wise. Nev thought they looked as boring as hell; he wouldn't want to eat them. Imagine getting all your nutrition from a pile of dry little biscuits? If that's all Peanut had been fed, no wonder he'd wolfed the chicken down. He'd eaten his biscuits too, but only after he'd scoffed the chicken first.

Peanut was a fast learner, and he'd soon cottoned on that when Nev opened the fridge, nice things came out of it. He was looking up at Nev expectantly right now, his tail wagging, his mouth open and tongue lolling, and when Nev put the chicken on the counter, the dog licked his lips.

Nev tore a small piece off. 'Peanut, sit,' he commanded, and to his immense surprise Peanut sat. Nev promptly gave him his reward, and the terrier gulped it down, not bothering to chew.

Well, well, well, Nev thought, *so he does know some basic commands*. Nev didn't know why he hadn't tried asking the dog to sit before now, and he wondered what else Peanut could do.

'Lie down.'

Peanut cocked his head to the side, his ears pricked. He was clearly trying to work out what Nev was saying.

'Lie *down*,' Nev repeated, emphasising the word down. That seemed to do the trick as Peanut shuffled his forelegs forward until he was in a prone position.

'Good boy!' Nev told him delightedly and gave him another morsel of chicken. 'Peanut, roll over,' he instructed.

Peanut stared at him.

'Roll over?' he repeated, this time making it sound more of a question than a command.

The dog continued to stare, and Nev guessed he hadn't been taught that trick.

With some chicken in one hand, Nev bent forward and held out his hand. 'Paw?'

Peanut duly obliged, slapping one small paw into Nev's open palm, then once again snaffling the morsel of food when it was offered.

Nev was elated. This was much more promising. He should have done this in the beginning. It probably wouldn't stop the barking, but if he could distract Peanut with food, it might help.

Typically, now that Nev was locked and loaded with a small bag of chicken about his person, Peanut didn't utter a peep. Not one little bark or whimper.

Feeling more confident about taking him out, Nev popped the harness on him, clipped his lead on and told him they were going for a walk. But they'd only just stepped outside the door when Peanut's hooligan tendency reared its head as a car drove past, and he let out a volley of ear-piercing barks.

'Stop that!' Nev cried, but Peanut ignored him, dancing around on the end of the lead, his tail stiff, his eyes following the car. The barking didn't cease until the vehicle was out of sight.

That was a new one on Nev; until now the dog had only reacted when he'd seen another canine. Why on earth should he lose his head over a small yellow hatchback? Then belatedly Nev realised that a dog's snout had been sticking out through the passenger window, and his heart sank. It seemed that even dogs in cars could set him off.

Filled with renewed tension, Nev marched the little dog along the road, flinching every time a vehicle went past, but Peanut thankfully didn't react. However, by the time they were halfway around the park loop, Peanut had had a hissy fit at three dogs and now had his sights set on a fourth. Unfortunately, distracting him with chicken hadn't worked, since the terrier hadn't given the treats a second glance, more intent on shrieking at every pooch he saw. The odd thing was, along with the frantic barking there was a great deal of pulling on the lead, bouncing around, and excited tail wagging.

The terrier's reaction appeared to be indiscriminate, but Nev was beginning to notice a pattern: Peanut had a beef with larger dogs, but only when they were some distance away. When they drew nearer, he was still excitable, but the closer they got the more his aggression waned.

'He's a live wire,' a lady with a fluffy Bichon Frise said. 'I could hear him from across the other side of the park.'

Nev's heart was in his mouth when she relinquished her tight grip on her pet's lead and the little dog trotted up to Peanut. Nev tensed, fully expecting Peanut to go berserk, but all he did was wag his tail and engage in some strategic sniffing.

'Well, I never!' he exclaimed. 'I felt sure he was going to go off on one. That's a good boy, Peanut.'

'Peanut? Aw, what a cute name! He must like Monty. Dogs are similar to us, I suppose, in that they like some people – or should I say *dogs* – and don't like others. We don't like everybody, do we? At least, *I* don't.' She pulled a face. 'That doesn't make me sound very nice, does it? What must you think of me?'

Nev tore his gaze away from the dogs, who were busy getting acquainted, and turned his attention to the Bichon's owner.

The woman was around sixty years of age, short, with curly brown hair, twinkling hazel eyes, and a friendly smile.

Nev took to her instantly. 'I can't be very nice either then, because I'm not too keen on some people,' he assured her, although he couldn't think of anyone he disliked off the top of his head. To be honest, at this very moment, he couldn't think of anything other than his dog's behaviour.

She bent down and offered Peanut her hand to sniff and when he gave her fingers a lick, she chuckled. 'Isn't he a friendly little soul. What was all that barking about, eh?'

Nev said wearily, 'That's what *I'd* like to know.'

'Has he always been shouty?'

'He's a rescue. I've only had him a few days and the dog sanctuary didn't know much about him because he was brought in as a stray.'

'Aw, bless him; he's probably just getting used to you and his new surroundings.'

'I hope so.' Nev's sigh was heartfelt.

When the woman laid a hand on his arm, Nev jumped. 'Promise me you'll give him every chance,' she pleaded. 'Monty was a rescue, and he was a nightmare when I first got him – he kept peeing in the kitchen.'

'Oh, dear,' Nev sympathised, relieved Peanut had known from the get-go that he had to do his business outside. And how had he let Nev know he wanted to go out? By barking, of course.

She removed her hand but her pleading expression remained. 'If you need to chat, you can usually find me in the park around this time,' she said.

Nev's eyes widened. Was she coming on to him? But as swiftly as the thought flew into his mind, it flew out again, as she continued, 'My partner is usually with me, but she's doing her stint as a volunteer in one of the charity shops in Thornbury – we're from there originally and have only recently moved to Picklewick – so it's just me today. But don't be afraid to come and say hello. My name's Sheila, by the way.'

'I'm Nev.'

'Nice to meet you, Nev. And you, too, Peanut. Bye.' And with a cheery wave she was on her way, leaving Nev to stare after her.

'She was nice,' he said to Peanut. Peanut's response was a quick wag of his tail.

Feeling more optimistic about Peanut meeting other dogs (and Nev meeting other dog walkers) they completed another lap of the park relatively incident free, except for a barking frenzy at a hound in the distance. Nev didn't feel as anxious this time though, especially since Peanut calmed down quickly. In fact, he seemed to deflate, as though the act of putting on a performance was the sole reason for barking in the first place. The behaviour was odd, but Nev thought he could work with it. Outside, at least. Indoors was a different matter. If he couldn't reduce Peanut's barking to more manageable levels at home, then...

Nev refused to complete the rest of that thought. Thankfully the house was detached (in the narrowest sense of the word, since the neighbours on both sides were only within arm-stretch distance), so at least there wasn't just a party wall between them and Peanut's nerve-shredding barks.

Relieved to be home, Nev sorted the dog out, then took off his shoes and padded through to the kitchen in his stocking feet, before realising he'd left his slippers at the bottom of the stairs. He had yet to get into a routine – they both did – but give it a bit of time and he'd work out a new way of doing things, such as coming and going via the utility door, for instance, to minimise the chance of messy, muddy paw prints. Since he'd gone to all the effort to clean and tidy the house, he wanted to try to keep on top of it.

As Nev put together supper for himself and Peanut, he found it comforting to have the dog around, even if Peanut did have a shout now and again. It was better than the silence that had echoed through the house since Tina had walked out.

But no matter how wonderful a companion Peanut was, the dog would never completely fill the gaping hole his wife had left in Nev's heart.

CHAPTER SEVEN

WHEN CLARISSA PHONED to invite Tina out for a drink on Friday evening, claiming that Tina hadn't been to The Black Horse for ages and that she had to bite the bullet at some point, Tina hadn't been convinced it was a good idea.

While she was getting ready to go out, dithering over what she should wear because she didn't want to appear to be making too much of an effort, she still wasn't convinced. And when she pushed open the pub's door, her ears assaulted by laughter and chatter at the same time as a waft of hops and whatever was on the specials board this evening assaulted her nose, she was downright convinced it was a bad idea.

But she was here now, so she may as well stay for a drink. If she didn't feel like having more than one, she didn't have to. *And you never know,* she thought, *I might enjoy it.* Hadn't she been complaining she felt lonely, so at least she'd be with other people tonight. Although Daphne was company in the house, the dog wasn't a substitute for another human being. The conversation tended to be a bit one-sided, for a start. No one could accuse Daphne of being the life and soul of the party. If Daphne were a person, she'd be the introvert sitting in the corner watching everything going on around her, but saying very little and refusing to get involved. There was nothing wrong with being an introvert, of course, but Tina felt she needed a little more liveliness to get her through the day.

She scanned the bar and spotted Clarissa and the rest of the gang in their usual corner. The "gang" consisted of four couples: it used to be five, but Tina walking out on Nev had put paid to that.

Quickly she counted heads – eight people at the table – and she breathed a sigh of relief that Nev wasn't there, before a bolt of longing hit her and she wished that he was. She didn't want to feel like a spare wheel, but that's what she was. The symmetry was gone. The group was out of balance and it needed someone else to even the numbers.

Clarissa saw her and waved her over. Tina wove her way across the room, faltering when she noticed that there were two empty seats around the table and not just one. Who else were they expecting?

Her heart sank as a thought occurred to her. *Please don't let them be setting me up on a blind date*, she prayed silently. She wouldn't put it past them, Clarissa especially.

Smiling tightly as she took a seat, Tina glanced across at the bar to Dave, the landlord, who mouthed, 'The usual?' at her, and she nodded.

Jillian, who was sitting to Clarissa's right, said, 'Hello stranger. I was beginning to think you'd left the country.'

Clarissa laughed. 'She did, but she came back. Had a wonderful time, didn't you, Tina?'

Tina made a kind of *yes I did face* whilst at the same time trying to give off an air of not wanting to talk about it. Let them make of it what they will.

Gordon, Jillian's fiancé (they'd been engaged ever since Tina had known them, but weren't showing any signs of getting married) said, 'I hear you've got a dog?'

Tina wasn't surprised he knew. Picklewick was a decent-sized village, but it was also small enough for gossip to quickly get around.

On safer territory, she answered, 'Yes, a greyhound. I got her from The Forever Home on Muddypuddle Lane.'

But before Gordon said, 'That's where you got *your* dog from, wasn't it, Nev?' Tina had already sensed that her husband was standing behind her.

Her heart gave a lurch. It was the feeling she used to get before they started going out together, when she fancied him rotten but didn't think he'd noticed her. Her heart used to do the same fluttery, stuttering thing whenever she caught sight of him, and it was doing it now, much to her consternation.

There wasn't time to analyse it, and she shuffled in her seat and looked away as he sat down.

'Hi,' he said, not looking at her.

'Hi.' She swallowed. 'How are you?'

'Fine thanks. You?'

'I'm good, thanks.' *Gosh, this is awkward*, she thought, wondering if she could make her excuses and leave.

Too late: Dave was bearing down on her with her drink and he also had one for Nev.

Tina picked up her glass and emptied half of it in one gulp. She should have asked for a double – and she would have if she'd realised the empty seat next to her had been for Nev. She wondered if he'd known she was going to be here, but from the way he was avoiding her gaze, she suspected not.

Gordon said, 'Isn't it funny how the pair of you both got dogs the minute you split up?'

Nothing like cutting right to the chase, Tina thought, grimacing. Feeling the need to justify herself, she said, 'Daphne, that's my dog, is better than a burglar alarm. She's very protective. In fact, I should have brought her with me this evening for the walk home.'

Clarissa laughed. 'Anyone would think Picklewick is a hotbed of criminal activity. You're as safe as houses here.'

Jillian said, 'I understand where she's coming from. A woman on her own feels vulnerable.'

'It's not that I feel *vulnerable*,' Tina protested, 'but there's no point in taking unnecessary risks.'

Fred, Clarissa's husband, scoffed. 'The only danger in this neck of the woods is going into a field with a bull in it, or having to reverse down one of the lanes because there's a tractor coming the other way.'

Clarissa asked, 'What about you, Nev? Why did you get a dog?'

Nev pointedly didn't look at Tina. 'It gets lonely in the house on your own.'

Tina took another mouthful of her drink. She'd give it five more minutes, then she'd leave. She wouldn't be lying when she said she had to get back to Daphne. Jakob had warned her the dog didn't do well being left on her own, and Tina didn't want to cause her any distress.

She could tell from the way Nev's shoulders were up around his ears and from the set of his jaw that he felt just as uncomfortable. She'd already suspected it might prove difficult to maintain a friendship with the women she'd known when she was part of a couple, and she wondered if Nev felt the same about the men. It was alright for him, she grumbled to herself: he'd always had more interests outside the home than her. She simply hadn't had the time. But with their eldest son now having relocated to Lincoln (she missed him terribly, and the grandchildren especially) and with Ryan leaving home, and then her recent retirement, she'd suddenly found she had time on her hands. Time she'd been dreaming about for years. Time she wanted to fill with doing exciting things with Nev.

Unfortunately, he hadn't had the same vision. He'd been content to do more of the same, day in, day out, until she wanted to scream in frustration.

While she'd been lost in her thoughts, the conversation had moved on and they were now talking about Clarissa and Fred's campervan. When Clarissa had first mentioned it, Tina had envisaged something like a VW camper, something cute and retro, but Clarissa and Fred had grander ideas. They weren't talking about a *van* – they were talking about an eight-berth motorhome. An entirely different prospect. Tina didn't think she'd feel comfortable handling one of those. Anyway, she wouldn't need the space, not for just her and Daphne. Something smaller that she could drive in and out of car parks without worrying about getting stuck, would do her.

Nev had turned away and was talking to Gordon about golf. He seemed quite knowledgeable from the snippets she could catch, which surprised her because he'd never shown an interest in the sport before. Maybe he was expanding his hobbies to fill his time?

'Of course, you need to get a habitation inspection done, as well as an MOT,' Clarissa was saying. 'Apparently, it's essential in order to keep the manufacturer's warranty valid, because they inspect the inside to make sure everything works correctly and is safe. And even if it's out of warranty, it's still a good idea to have one done.'

'Would that apply to something like a VW camper van?' Tina asked curiously.

'I would have thought so. Why? Are you thinking of getting one?'

'I might,' Tina mused. She had visions of her and Daphne waking up on a secluded beach, hearing nothing but waves and seagulls. She could tour Scotland, and maybe even go as far as the Outer Hebrides. She'd heard it was beautiful there. She'd still have the same problem of not having anyone to share it with though, but she'd have her dog for company and at least she'd see something of the world before it was too late.

A pang struck her in the solar plexus and she bit back a groan. If only Nev had been more adventurous. Meeting her halfway would have done it, but until she'd told him she was leaving, he hadn't been prepared to budge an inch. And afterwards his change of heart had come too late, since it had been born out of desperation.

Her gaze flickered to her husband, her eyes tracing the familiar lines of his face, still handsome despite the years, and her heart ached for what they could have had and for what might have been. They'd been good together once. Heck, they'd been *brilliant*. But somewhere along the way they'd become *un*coupled, their wants and needs diverging.

Oh, Nev...

She missed him so much, but she feared she missed the man he'd once been – not the man he had become. Anyway, whether she missed him or not was irrelevant now. It was too late to go back; Ryan had more or less told her that Nev wanted a divorce.

Had her husband really moved on? She didn't want to believe it, but then he probably hadn't wanted to believe it of *her,* either.

Tina's thoughts were interrupted by the arrival of one of her former neighbours, who gave her a tight smile of acknowledgement, then tapped Nev on the shoulder. When he bent down to speak to him, Tina tried to catch what he was saying but there was too much noise.

Whatever it was, made Nev shake his head and get to his feet with a frown. Draining the last of his pint, he was gone without so much as a backward glance, striding out of the pub on those long legs of his. And all Tina could do was watch him leave and wonder how she'd managed to make such a mess of things.

SO MANY EMOTIONS were swirling through Nev's mind as he stomped home from the pub that he didn't know where to begin. For a start, there was the dismay he'd felt at having his neighbour approach him in the pub to tell him that his dog was making a racket. That's what he *should* be focusing on, but he was also embarrassed because of how awkward he'd felt sitting next to Tina this evening. It hadn't been for long, barely fifteen minutes, but he wouldn't want to repeat the experience.

He blamed Fred for inviting him. Not that Nev needed an invitation – he could go to The Black Horse whenever he chose to – but he tended to avoid Friday nights because that's when the gang usually got together. He'd met one or two of the lads separately, but he hadn't wanted to risk bumping into Tina, even though both Fred and Gordon had assured him they hadn't seen her in the pub since the split.

He strongly suspected he'd been set up, and from the look on Tina's face when she saw him, he believed she hadn't been aware he'd be there, either.

His friends were wasting their time, if that was the case. By walking out, Tina had made it perfectly clear their marriage was over. So he had no idea what they were playing at. Aside from feeling embarrassed and annoyed, he also felt unbelievably sad. How could thirty-four years of marriage have come to this? The way she'd looked at him...

Nev hitched in a breath, the ache in his chest unbearable. All that talk of camper vans had cemented what he'd already suspected – that it wasn't his lack of enthusiasm for exotic places and expensive food that had made her walk out; it was because she didn't love him anymore.

I mean, you could hardly drive to Goa in a camper van, he thought. And although there were some lovely places in the UK (he deliberately tried not to think of his suggestion they go to Clacton-on-Sea) none of them would be as exotic as the places she'd mentioned to him. Ergo, she had lied to him. Knowing Tina, she'd probably been trying to let him down gently; if you call walking out with two full suitcases and several bags full of her possessions, *gently*.

And one thing she'd said kept playing over and over in his mind – *'love doesn't come into it'*. She'd wanted a fresh start without him, that was all, but he wished she'd had the guts to tell him so, because it might have made it easier to move on. Although *moving on* was a dim and distant prospect, since if he couldn't have Tina, he didn't want anyone.

As he reached his front door, he was beginning to think he didn't want Peanut, either. The dog's yipping could clearly be heard, and for a minute he was tempted to turn around and walk away, just to see how long the blasted animal could keep it up.

Nev couldn't be that callous, though. He'd been reading up on the topic, and for dogs to bark like that meant something was wrong. There must be some need that Nev wasn't meeting. Maybe it had been too soon to leave Peanut on his own? But he'd only intended to be out for an hour, and he'd been out much less than that. Next time – if there would ever *be* a next time – he'd take Peanut with him since dogs were allowed in The Black Horse; but it didn't solve the problem of when he went to bowls, or he went to Thornbury to do his monthly shop. And what if he needed to get his hair cut, or go to the dentist, or the doctor? Luckily none of those things were imminent, so he had a bit of time. And he *had* promised to give the dog time.

Putting the key in the lock, he pushed open the front door to be met by an airborne ball of white and tan terrier.

Peanut was only small, but the force of his leap made Nev stagger back and he automatically wrapped his arms around the little creature to prevent the dog from falling. Peanut wriggled and squirmed, trying to lick Nev's face, making happy little whimpers, and Nev hadn't received such a joyous welcome in his life, not even from the kids when they were little.

He suddenly realised what people meant when they say "you can't beat the love of a good dog".

It might just be relief on Peanut's part because someone had come back for him and he hadn't been abandoned again (*if* that's what had happened to him previously) but Nev couldn't help reading human emotion on the dog's happy face.

'I'm here, boy, I'm here,' he muttered, putting Peanut down. 'No need for you to get so upset. Let's make a deal, shall we? You try not to bark so much, and I'll try to be a more understanding dog parent. How does that sound?'

Peanut trotted at his heels, his wet nose touching Nev's ankle as he went into the kitchen to let the dog out in case he needed a wee. But the enthusiastic and joyous welcome aside, Nev's sadness was acute. The very, *very* faint hope he'd been harbouring that Tina had got herself a dog for the exact same reason he had, was now scuppered. She'd acquired a dog as some form of protection or deterrent for when she was on the road in this camper van she was talking about buying, *not* because she was lonely.

He'd lost her. *He really had lost her.*

CHAPTER EIGHT

SOME PEOPLE TEND to be quieter than others, more introspective and more withdrawn. Dogs must be the same, Tina concluded, because Daphne was all of those things. There was also something else bothering Tina: she suspected Daphne was sad. Without knowing her background, it was impossible to say why this could be, but she desperately hoped it wasn't because the dog was pining for her previous owner.

Still, after three weeks together, they'd fallen into an easy routine, and Daphne had appeared to settle in. She had her favourite spot on the couch where she liked to cuddle, and although Tina had been tempted to let her sleep with her,

Daphne had her own comfy bed in the corner of the bedroom. After so many years of sharing with Nev, it didn't feel right to share a bed with anyone else, even if it was a dog. Anyway, Daphne was too restless; she managed to disturb Tina a couple of times at night as it was. Imagine if the dog was lying next to her? Tina wouldn't get a wink of sleep!

Despite believing greyhounds needed a lot of exercise, she was surprised to find that Daphne didn't. The dog loved being outdoors and she loved going out on walks, but it seemed that the amount of time she spent outside was more important to her than the distance walked. She was perfectly happy to plod around the park for an hour, and although she enjoyed longer walks, they didn't appear to be essential.

Today's walk was going to be of the longer variety, because Tina had set her sights on visiting the farm shop on Muddypuddle Lane. She'd heard some good things about their ice cream, and they also had handmade soaps and all kinds of other goodies. She had a small rucksack with her to carry her purchases home, and if she wanted to buy more than she could carry, she could always return later with the car.

It was the tail end of summer, just before the kids went back to school, and autumn had yet to bite although the season was already making its presence felt in the shortening of the days, the apples ripening on the trees, and the glossy blackberries peeping out of the hedgerows. Early morning and late evening were chilly, but the days themselves were a pleasant temperature, and Tina was looking forward to the walk.

She had invested in a pair of hiking boots, perfect for traversing muddy paths, fields, and rocky tracks on the mountainside, and as soon as Daphne saw her put them on, she began prancing around with high delicate steps. The dog moved with grace and elegance, all curved lines and light on her paws. Tina fancifully mused that greyhounds were the ballerinas of the dog world. She could be goofy too – the dog, not Tina – and had been known to bounce around like a puppy wanting to play on occasion. That was when Tina saw a different side to her, a younger, more lighthearted side, and she wished she was like that more often. But it wasn't in Daphne's nature, and Tina was just grateful she was gentle and calm for most of the time.

Tina had heard on the grapevine that Nev's dog was a right little bruiser; a Jack Russell terrier apparently, and noisy with it. She wondered how he was coping, then with a sigh, she pushed thoughts of her husband from her mind. She'd found herself doing that a lot lately. An almost impossible task in the middle of the night, but easier when she had something to occupy her, such as the prospect of taking Daphne for a walk, for instance.

Her little rented cottage was on the opposite side of the village to Muddypuddle Lane, which meant she had to walk along the high street and out the other side. It was around nine-thirty, and predictably busy. Picklewick might be small, but it had a nice selection of artisan shops, as well as the café and the pub, and as she strolled along the pavement in no particular hurry, she smiled and said hello to several familiar faces. A few even stopped to pet Daphne, and Tina felt that she was becoming known as Daphne's mum, rather than Nev's wife.

Or should she call herself his *ex-wife*?

The two of them were currently in limbo; still married, yet no longer together. From what Ryan had hinted, Tina was surprised not to have received a solicitor's letter informing her that Nev had begun divorce proceedings, but perhaps he didn't feel quite up to it yet. She knew *she* didn't. She was dreading it. Divorce sounded so final, but really, *what* had she *expected?* Walking out on him was only the beginning of a road which ended in a decree absolute. She'd taken the first step, but she wasn't entirely sure she wanted to take the next one. Maybe Nev felt the same?

She hadn't seen him since that Friday evening in the pub, and she wondered how he was. He'd lost weight, she'd noticed, and his sparkle had disappeared. His expression had been closed and flat, and he'd held himself as though he'd received a painful blow, which she supposed he had. It made her feel sick to think *she* had caused it. If she could turn the clock back, would she have stayed and tried to make a go of things?

Hell yes.

She was now on the other side of the village where the houses were further apart and set back off the road, reminding her of her own house. Not hers any longer; technically yes, but morally no. What would happen to it when they did get a divorce, she asked herself. She supposed they'd split everything equally down the middle. She had a vague idea of what the house might be worth, and out of her share she could buy a nice camper van, one with a cute name, and still have a fair bit left over, possibly enough to buy a small place like the one she was renting. Or she could just live in the van.

It was a thought. She'd seen ones with tiny wood burners, solar panels on the roof, and a proper loo and shower. She could leave Picklewick and spend the rest of her life on the road, doing what she wanted to do – travel, and there was nothing stopping her from crossing the channel and exploring Europe. Nothing, except for the fear of doing it on her own. Because she *would* be on her own, even with Daphne. She'd have no one to bounce ideas off, or to share her worries with, or to celebrate the joys with.

Don't be a wimp, she told herself silently. Other women did it; she knew this because she followed a few of them on social media, or she'd come across their blogs. There was even one brave soul who backpacked *everywhere*: she'd sold her house, her car, and all her possessions, and was walking the world.

Tina didn't have that kind of courage. She enjoyed her luxuries too much, such as a nice bed, for instance. Maybe a VW camper van would be too small to live in for an extended period? Perhaps she should look at something larger? Not too *much* larger though, because she was worried about manoeuvring it.

The kissing gate at the start of the field leading towards the stables on Muddypuddle Lane made a satisfying clunk as it shut behind her and Daphne. Tina would have loved to let the dog off the lead, but she was scared she wouldn't come back when she was called, but at least the lead was an extendable one, so Tina let it play out, happy for the dog to take her time. There was no rush, so they could dawdle as much as they wanted.

The field sloped upwards towards the stables, and although sometimes horses grazed there, it was currently empty of livestock. The grass had been allowed to grow and reached her hips, golden waves rippling incessantly in the breeze. Grasshoppers chirped unseen amongst the long stalks, and the piping call of a curlew made her glance up at the sky but all she could see was the fork tailed silhouette of a red kite as it circled overhead. It was so peaceful up here, and she felt some of her tension fall away. She should do this more often, she thought, and now she had Daphne, there was no excuse not to.

Tina took a breath of warm, scented air and carried on walking, Daphne at her side. The dog stopped to sniff every now and then, and Tina was content to wander at the dog's pace. When they reached the top of the field and the next gate, Tina ruffled Daphne's ears and told her she was a good girl. Daphne gave her a look as if to say, *Yes, I know I am,* which made Tina laugh.

As the path passed near to the stables, Daphne's nose began to twitch, and Tina soon discovered why when the unmistakable scent of horse reached her. It wasn't a nasty smell, just an unfamiliar one. She'd never ridden, but she'd attended a summer fete here a couple of years back and remembered stroking their soft velvety noses and being awed at the size of the animals.

The farm lay further up the lane beyond the stables, and Tina remembered it as being a sheep farm once upon a time.

Apparently it now specialised in goats, which was where the ice cream and the soap came from. Dulcie Fairfax made the soap, and her partner, Otto, was responsible for the ice cream, both of which were made from goats' milk. Otto also owned The Wild Side, a Michelin star restaurant in Picklewick. It had been open a while, but despite Tina suggesting they try it out, Nev hadn't been keen so they'd never gone. And she wouldn't go on her own now obviously, but she'd heard that some of the food on the menu was available in the farm shop, so she vowed to treat herself if she saw something she fancied. It would be the nearest she'd get to dining at the restaurant, she thought sadly.

The final push up Muddypuddle Lane was the steepest, the road itself being narrow, potholed and lined by hedges on either side. Through gaps in the foliage she could see horses grazing, their tails peacefully flicking as they blew the occasional horsey snort through their nostrils.

Daphne was practically pulling Tina up the hill in her eagerness to get to wherever they were going, and Tina wondered if she remembered it from when she was brought here, but surmised that she probably didn't. And the dog certainly hadn't been thriving in the sanctuary, so it wasn't as though she was eager to return. She was probably just enjoying being somewhere different, with new sights, sounds and smells – and Tina had to admit there were plenty of smells. The breeze carried the occasional whiff of horse, along with some kind of sheepy aroma which she assumed was from the goats, as well as the scent of the wildflowers in the hedgerows.

It might be lovely now, but Tina couldn't help wonder what it might be like to live up here in the depths of winter, especially if there was snow down. She could imagine it being very pretty though, and she made a note to remind herself to bring Daphne up here as soon as it snowed. She'd have to get the dog a nice warm coat, she decided, and made a note to pop into the pet shop soon to see if they had anything suitable. There was no point in waiting until the bad weather arrived: she liked to be prepared.

It suddenly struck her that her vision of bringing Daphne up here in the snow mightn't come to fruition if she did, in fact, buy a small motorhome. They could very well be in the south of France, or Italy, or anywhere warmer than Picklewick on a damp and chilly November morning. But although she was still toying with the idea, something was holding her back, and it wasn't just fear of jumping in with both feet and then regretting it. She'd already done that once this year.

At the entrance to the farm a stone trough filled to the brim with late summer flowers grabbed her attention, and she gazed around her with interest. The cobbled farmyard had a barn and other buildings on the left, and a grey stone house at the far end with a gorgeous view out over the valley. What a wonderful place to live, she thought enviously, as she eyed a sign for an orchard and another for a goat meadow.

Bleating noises coming from one of the barns caught Daphne's attention, as did the chickens roaming free, and Tina tightened her grip on the lead. It wouldn't do for Daphne to go haring after them, and although she was good with other dogs, Tina had no way of knowing how she might react around livestock.

Seeing an open door with a *Farm Shop* sign above it, she headed towards it, then hesitated, wondering what she should do with Daphne.

A shadowy figure inside called out, 'It's okay, you can bring your dog in. We don't mind animals here.'

Relieved, Tina stepped into the relative gloom and it took a moment for her eyes to adjust from the brightness of the day outside. When they did, she saw shelves stocked with soaps and candles, jars of honey, pots of jams and chutneys, and fresh produce and eggs, along with a chiller laden with bottles of milk, cheeses, pastries and savoury items, and even ready meals and soups. A sign announced that everything was fresh and homemade on the premises. Tina didn't know where to start – it all looked so wholesome.

Then her eyes came to rest on a poster advertising a secure dog walking field at The Forever Home, and she smiled. It looked like her wish might be answered, and if she could book a session, she might be able to let Daphne off the lead after all.

A woman was stocking a shelf with punnets of fat purple blackberries, glossy and mouthwatering, and Tina realised she knew her.

'Bea, hi, I didn't realise you worked here.' Bea was the same age as Tina's eldest son, and the two had been in the same class in Picklewick's little primary school. She was all grown up now, of course, with a family of her own.

Bea smiled. 'I thought it was you. How are you, Tina? And who is this?' Her gaze dropped to the dog.

'This is Daphne. We thought we'd take a walk up to the farm and have a look around the shop.'

'Feel free,' Bea said. 'As you can see, we've got fresh blackberries, handpicked this morning, and so are the pears. We'll have apples soon, but they're not quite ready yet. I keep telling people that you need to pop in on a weekly basis, because the produce changes all the time depending on what's in season. In case you're wondering, this week's ice cream flavours are raspberry, honey, or rose hip – or why don't you try all three!'

It all looked fresh and delicious, and Tina was spoilt for choice. She wanted one of everything, but she knew she'd never manage to eat it all on her own. But the fact that the products changed so regularly meant she'd have a perfect excuse to come back soon.

Feeling peckish, even though breakfast hadn't been very long ago, she wandered over to the chiller section and her gaze was snagged by a freshly prepared meal of roast chicken with sweet chestnuts and wild mushrooms in a creamy sauce.

Automatically she picked up two portions, thinking they would be perfect for her and Nev's tea this evening, and then it hit her.

There *was* no her and Nev. She'd made sure of that. And then she couldn't hold back the tears as they welled up and spilled down her cheeks.

She must have looked a right sight standing there holding two ready meals and sobbing, but she couldn't seem to stop.

Bea hurried over. 'What's wrong?'

Tina hitched in a shaky breath and managed to say, 'Nev,' before the sobs regained their hold.

'Nev? Nothing's happened to him, has it?' Bea asked anxiously.

'He's fine,' Tina wailed.

Bea put her arm around her. 'That's good, isn't it?'

'He thinks I don't love him.'

Bea handed Tina a tissue, which Tina gratefully accepted, dabbing at her eyes and then blowing her nose. 'Come and sit down, and I'll make us a cup of tea.' She led her to the counter and pulled out a stool.

Tina perched on it, conscious of Daphne's reassuring nose on her leg. The dog whined, and Tina's chin wobbled again. 'I'm sorry, Daphne, I didn't mean to upset you.'

Bea placed a mug of builder's tea on the counter, together with a sugar bowl and a spoon. 'Do you want to talk about it?'

Tina, her eyes firmly on the mug, bit her lip. There was no point. What was done, was done, and talking about it wouldn't change a thing.

'It might help if you get it off your chest. They say a problem shared is a problem halved,' Bea suggested. 'Although I've never been sure of the accuracy of that.'

Tina blurted, 'You know that me and Nev have split up?' When Bea nodded, she continued, 'It was my fault. I left him because I wanted some excitement.'

'Did you find any?'

Miserably, she shook her head. 'The only thing I've found is loneliness.'

'Do you regret leaving him?'

'Yes.' Her voice was barely above a whisper.

'Because you still love him? Or because you don't want to be lonely?'

Tina shot her a glance: it was a perceptive question. 'Both,' she replied honestly. 'I've never stopped loving him. I just didn't love what he'd become. I wanted to live a little. Now that we'd both retired and the kids don't need us, I wanted to do something different, something fun, something just for the two of us.'

'What did Nev want?'

Again, another pertinent question. 'He was happy with the way things were.'

'Is he happy now?'

Tina winced. That was below the belt, but before she could respond, Bea carried on, 'Are *you* happy now?'

'No, I'm not.' She jerked her thumb at the chiller and the two chicken meals resting on the top. 'I almost bought those for our tea, and then I remembered.'

'How long is it been? Have you given it enough time?'

'I've given it *too* much time,' Tina replied. 'I must have been out of my mind believing that the grass is greener. It's nothing but a bloody wilderness.'

When Bea blinked, Tina wondered whether she was being overly dramatic.

Bea said, 'Is it too late? Might there be a chance the two of you could get back together?'

'He won't want me back after what I did. I hurt him so badly. He's not going to want to risk that again.'

'Retirement is a big adjustment,' Bea said. 'It's like any life stage, it takes a while to get used to.'

'But that's the problem!' Tina cried. 'I don't *want* to get used to it anymore. I want my old life back. I want *Nev*. I want for this never to have happened.'

'You can't turn the clock back,' Bea pointed out reasonably, 'but if you really want things to go back to the way they were, you need to tell him. I take it you haven't?' she checked.

'I haven't.' Tina's reply was mournful.

'Don't you think you should?'

'What if he tells me to bugger off?'

'Then at least you know where you stand,' was Bea's prompt response. 'After all, what have you got to lose since you believe you've lost it already?'

Tina dabbed at her cheeks again. The tissue had become shredded and soggy, and her throat was dry, so she took a sip of her tea, then said, 'I didn't *lose* it – I threw it away.'

'Then you need to get it back again.'

CHAPTER NINE

'FOR PETE'S SAKE, Peanut, you're not a husky and I'm not a sled,' Nev told the terrier, who was pulling on his harness for all he was worth, attempting to tow Nev along the street in the same manner a tug pulled a tanker. The power to weight ratio was probably the same as well, Nev thought, wondering what had got the dog so worked up.

He hadn't been like this when they'd stepped outside the door this morning, but as soon as they'd reached the high street, he'd got a bee in his bonnet and decided there was somewhere he wanted to be. Unfortunately for Peanut, where *he* wanted to go didn't appear to be the same place that *Nev* wanted to go.

Nev had his sights set on the newsagents, to buy a paper, then he'd take Peanut for a stroll around the park before returning home. It wasn't the news he was after particularly; it was the crossword. He found he quite liked attempting to complete it over lunch. He'd read somewhere about keeping one's brain active, and since he was now keeping his body more active he thought it was high time he gave his mind the same care.

The chap who ran the newsagents was getting used to seeing him with Peanut, and didn't mind him bringing the dog in. As a general rule, Nev scooped the dog up and tucked him under his arm, mainly because he didn't trust the little so-and-so to behave himself. Especially today, because Peanut really seemed to have it on him. He was barking a lot too, but not his normal ear-piercing bark of excitement

– these were little yips and yelps, and Nev wasn't certain what they meant.

Resigning himself to never finding out, Nev reined him in once they reached the newsagent, and picked him up.

Peanut took exception and began to wriggle.

'You know the drill,' Nev reminded him. 'You don't go down until we come back out.'

Almost as if he understood, Peanut subsided, hanging limply as though all the fight had gone out of him. But Nev wasn't fooled. He knew the dog was biding his time.

Newspaper acquired, Nev lowered Peanut to the pavement as soon as they were outside, expecting him to dart ahead and pull on his lead the way he normally did (this dog had yet to work out what heel meant), but was surprised when he hung back and tried to tug Nev in the opposite direction.

Two doors up from the newsagents was the butchers, and Nev guessed that's where the dog wanted to go, egged on by the enticing smell of the large marrow bones which were in a box on the pavement outside to tempt Picklewick's canine residents.

'No chance, matey,' Nev said. 'We're going to the park. No bones for you today – you've still got one at home you haven't finished gnawing on.'

Peanut sat down and refused to budge, despite Nev gently pulling on the lead. Not wanting to resort to dragging him, there was only one thing for it: he'd have to pick him up again.

'This is supposed to be a walk, not a carry,' he told Peanut, who looked up at him and whined. 'If you think I'm going to be carrying you everywhere, you're sadly mistaken,' he added as the dog went limp again.

Hoping Peanut had seen sense, Nev placed him on the pavement once more. It was a mistake, because the dog immediately tried to head off in the opposite direction.

Nev scooped him up again. 'You really are being naughty today,' he admonished, but his tone was kind. This little fella had a mind of his own and was definitely a character.

Nev had been doing some reading, and had discovered that terriers could be quite independent and stubborn, as well as being single-minded. Peanut had obviously got something in his head, but hopefully, he would get whatever it was out of his system by the time they reached the park. There would be so many smells, and hopefully a few dogs to bark at to distract him.

He was getting better on the barking front, Nev acknowledged, as he walked along the road leading to the park gate. Peanut tended to only shout at dogs he didn't recognise now, and had no problem with the regulars he met most days. Nev still didn't fully trust him (even though there didn't appear to be a nasty bone in his body) so he wasn't taking any chances. He wished he could let him off his lead, but as well as being concerned about his reaction to other dogs, Nev wasn't confident he would come back when he was called. One of the people Nev had met recently had mentioned that The Forever Home had a secure field which could be rented out by the hour, so maybe he'd look into it. He would dearly love to play fetch with him and the dog deserved to have a good run around. He'd give The Forever Home a call when he got home, he decided, thinking maybe Peanut wasn't getting enough exercise, and ball chasing would wear him out.

Peanut continued to play up even after the first circuit of the park (Nev normally did three laps) which generally took about forty-five minutes in total, but was taking longer because the dog was continually hanging back.

'Don't you want to go for a walk today? Is that it? Do you want to go home?' Nev asked him.

Peanut sat on his haunches.

'What if we find a bench to sit on for a little while? We can watch the world go by and then if you still want to go home, we'll go home.'

One of these days that dog is going to answer me, Nev mused. *Or perhaps I'm just going to imagine he does*. He was spending an ordinate amount of time talking to the dog, and he wondered if this was normal. Did other people speak to their dogs the way he spoke to Peanut? He suspected not. Oh well, he mused sadly, it was better than talking to himself.

'We'll sit on this bench right here,' he said. It was placed at the junction between two paths and had a good view of each. It also had a good view of several pigeons pecking about in the recently mown grass, and a squirrel, who froze when it caught sight of them. He'd have thought Peanut would be interested in birds and squirrels, but he didn't bat an eyelid, not even when the squirrel broke cover and darted up the nearest tree. The only thing Peanut was interested in was other dogs, and even that had mostly subsided. Yet he always seemed to be on high alert, and Nev had no clue why.

Remembering the paper under his arm, Nev unfolded it and glanced at the headlines. Doom, gloom, celebrity gossip, and more doom. Par for the course really, he thought, skimming the main story. Thankfully Peanut had stopped insisting that Nev go in the direction *he* wanted to go and was now quietly lying underneath the bench, so Nev turned the page and continued reading.

It was actually quite civilised sitting in the park on a warm summer morning, with the birds chirping and the bees buzzing around in the flowerbeds. The only thing that would make it nicer would be if there were a café here. He could imagine sitting there with a cup of coffee, reading his newspaper, with his dog by his—

Something didn't feel right.

Nev glanced around, wondering what it was, and then, with dread, he realised there was nothing on the end of the lead. It had been chewed clean through! All he had in his hand was half a leather lead, and Peanut was nowhere in sight.

Nev leapt to his feet.

'Peanut!' he shouted, *'Peanut!'* as he scanned the flower bed, the spaces between the trees, and the path.

There was no sign of the dog.

Beginning to panic, Nev cupped his hands around his mouth and yelled once more. 'Peanut! Come here, boy!'

Still nothing. His head cocked, Nev listened intently, hoping to hear a telltale bark, but the only sounds were the birds and the gentle breeze rustling the leaves overhead.

'Peanut!' He was shouting at the top of his voice now. *'Peanut! Where are you?'*

Nev looked down at the chewed end of the lead. This wasn't simply a dog wandering off. This was a bid for freedom. But why? Hadn't Nev been good to him? He fed him, he walked him, he *loved* him. What more could a dog want?

The high street! Peanut had been trying to tell him something, and in hindsight he didn't think the dog had wanted to visit the butchers. Nev had no idea where the dog had wanted to go, but Peanut had been adamant. Nev should have listened to him, but...

He began to run, his feet pounding the path, his arms pumping. He didn't know how long he'd be able to keep this up (he hadn't gone more than a few steps and he was already out of breath), but he had to find him before something awful happened. Peanut could get lost or…

Nev didn't want to complete that thought, and as he dashed through the park, he berated himself for choosing a bench at the furthest point from the gates. But he couldn't run any faster, and certainly not as fast as Peanut. The dog could be half a mile away or more by now. What kind of dog parent— ?

Nev slowed, squinting. Was that Sheila?

He narrowed his eyes.

It was, and she had a familiar little creature in her arms. Relief flooded through him, and his pounding heart skipped a beat. *She'd found Peanut.*

He hurried up to her, breathless and shaken. 'Oh, thank god!' he panted. 'You found him. Is he alright?'

'He's fine, but are *you?*' she asked, her gaze raking his face as she handed Peanut over.

Peanut, oblivious to the commotion he'd caused, gave Nev a swift lick on the cheek, and Nev held the solid little body close and buried his nose in the dog's neck. Now that the adrenaline was starting to wear off, he was beginning to feel decidedly shaky. It occurred to him just how much the dog had come to mean to him, and he'd be devastated if anything happened to the little pooch.

'The blighter chewed through his lead. I don't know where he thought he was going. Where did you find him?'

'On Blackthorne Road. He was going hell for leather and it was sheer luck that somebody was coming out of their house as he was racing past and they tripped over him. They weren't hurt thankfully, but it slowed him enough for me to grab hold of him. If you don't mind me saying, you look a bit grey. Are you sure you're okay?' she asked again.

'I blame myself. I only took my eyes off him for a second.' Nev shook his head.

Sheila took charge. 'Come on, we're going to the pet shop to get a stronger lead for this little man, and then we're going to have a nice cup of tea. I think you could do with one.'

Nev was more than happy to comply, and when they reached the café and she ushered him inside, he sank gratefully into one of the chairs at a table near the window, while Sheila hurried off to the pet shop to make the purchase.

She was back in no time with a brand-new lead and a couple of doggy treats.

'There,' she said, 'no harm done,' as Nev clipped the new lead (a long metal chain with a leather loop at the holding end) onto the terrier's harness. 'Let's see him chew through *that,*' she announced in satisfaction.

Peanut gave her a disgusted look but accepted the biscuit. With the dogs lying companionably underneath the table, Sheila ordered a pot of tea for two and a couple of slices of cake. 'You need the sugar,' she informed him. 'You've had a shock.'

She was right, Nev conceded: he *had* had a shock. 'He's a naughty little sod,' he grumbled as he brought out his wallet to reimburse her for the lead and to pay for the drinks. 'He's been nothing but trouble since the day I brought him home. But I wouldn't be without him now.'

Sheila leant across the table and put her hand over his. 'They do tend to worm their way into our hearts,' she agreed. 'But don't beat yourself up. It's not your fault. They've got minds of their own and some can be more determined than others.'

'I don't know what got into him,' Nev said, 'but I had the feeling he was trying to run away from me.'

'Nonsense!' she exclaimed. 'He's just a typical terrier. Once they get an idea in their head there's no budging it. He'd clearly caught the scent of something and was off. That's why they make such good ratters.' She gave his hand another squeeze and smiled.

Nev nodded and smiled back. 'You're right, but he didn't half give me a shock. Thank you for finding him.' Then he leant forward and gave her a peck on the cheek, overcome with gratitude.

'No need to thank me – you'd do the same if you saw a dog on its own.'

Nev would, but he couldn't help feeling dreadful, nonetheless. Not only hadn't he been able to hold on to his wife, it seemed he couldn't hang onto his dog, either.

EMBARRASSED DIDN'T begin to cover it.
Tina was mortified. She couldn't believe
she'd broken down in public like that.
Okay, so it had only been in front of one
person, but that wasn't the point. She
knew Bea, but not well, and certainly not
well enough to blubber all over her. It was
so unlike her, but in a way it had been
cathartic. Especially when Bea had
suggested she speak to Nev and tell him
how she felt. As Bea had quite rightly
pointed out, what did she have to lose?
Her self-respect maybe, but it was a small
price to pay for what she might gain if she
came clean and confessed she'd made the
biggest mistake of her life and begged him
for another chance.

The thought of speaking to her husband
terrified her in case he rejected her, but
she really didn't have an awful lot of

choice. She had to know if he'd take her back, and the only way was to talk to him.

As she slowly made her way down the lane and through the field, Daphne trotting by her side, Tina practised what she was going to say.

'Nev, I'm sorry, I've made a terrible mistake,' she said out loud. Would that do as a start? Should she blurt it out like that? Or should she ask him how he was and build up to it gradually?

That probably wasn't the best idea. She needed to just tell him. If she bumped into him on the street and asked how he was, that would be one thing, and perhaps she could lead up to a *I've made a total balls of things, can you forgive me* kind of conversation. But turning up at his house and just randomly asking if he was okay, wouldn't work. Anyway, she couldn't rely on bumping into him; even though Picklewick was small, she couldn't guarantee their paths would cross anytime soon.

Therefore the only reasonable thing to do was to be grown up about it and go round there this evening. If he kept the same routine, he'd probably be eating his tea between six and six thirty, so she'd wait until seven o'clock and hope he'd be in. Aside from the occasional visit to the pub, Nev didn't used to go out much in the evenings. He might have changed his habits, of course, but as she had no way of knowing she'd have to take a chance.

Tina rolled her shoulders, the rucksack's straps weighing her down, and berated herself for buying so much; but she'd felt obliged to after sobbing all over Bea's countertop. Anyway, the food wouldn't go to waste. She'd munch her way through it eventually – or, if everything went to plan, she'd be able to share it with Nev.

It made her heart race to think she might be moving back into their marital home shortly. Maybe tomorrow, if he welcomed her with open arms. Mind you, Nev had never been one for spontaneity, so he'd probably want a while to think about it and she wouldn't blame him. After the way she'd treated him, he'd be a saint to take her back, so it was only to be expected that he'd be wary.

With her mind totally preoccupied with thoughts of her husband, Tina hadn't taken much notice of Daphne on the walk home, but as they went through the kissing gate at the end of the field leading to the outskirts of the village, she noticed the dog seemed a little down, although it was difficult to tell with a greyhound. They normally carried their heads and tails quite low, but Daphne's was positively drooping.

'You okay, girl?'

Daphne glanced up at her, only her eyes and expressive eyebrows moving, and Tina could have sworn the dog was saying, *What do you think?*

'Did you want a longer walk? Is that it? Or did my crying upset you? Sorry if it did, but I'm alright now, I promise.'

It was a lie. She wasn't alright and she wouldn't be until she'd spoken to Nev. And even then, she still mightn't be okay. It all depended on how the conversation went.

As she approached the high street, Tina hoped she didn't look as though she'd been crying and wished she'd thought to bring her sunglasses, but if she kept her head down and concentrated on where she was walking, she wouldn't have to meet anyone's eye and hopefully no one would be any the wiser.

Her stride purposeful in order to deter random chat, she marched briskly along the pavement. With any luck, people would think she was late for an appointment or had somewhere important to be, and they wouldn't bother her.

Tina was mid-stride when Daphne halted abruptly, catching her unawares, and she staggered slightly at the sudden dead weight on the end of the lead. Assuming that the dog had got snagged on something – it had happened once before when Tina had gone one way around a lamppost and Daphne had gone the other, and occasionally Daphne came to a standstill when there was an interesting smell that would prove hard to drag her away from – Tina glanced behind and was surprised to see the dog standing perfectly still with her head up and her nose in the air, sniffing.

Oh goodness, what can she smell now, she wondered. She'd never come across such a sniffy dog. Anyone would think she had some bloodhound in her, Tina grumbled to herself. Daphne should have had a career as a sniffer dog for the police or Customs, she thought, tugging on the lead and urging the dog to move.

Daphne was having none of it. With all four paws planted firmly on the pavement, she leant back, using her body as a counterweight to Tina's pulling.

Not wanting to hurt her, Tina thought she'd give her a second to get whatever it was out of her system. The dog's head was turning from side to side, her sensitive nose twitching, and Tina glanced around to see what might be causing such a reaction. Of course, there was the butchers which they'd just passed, but—

Then she saw him. *Nev.*

He was sitting in the café with a woman and they were gazing into each other's eyes and smiling, and they were *holding hands.*

Tina blinked in disbelief. That couldn't be Nev.

Could it?

It bloody looked like him. And who was he with?

The woman seemed familiar but Tina couldn't think where she'd seen her before. She was certainly being overly familiar with Nev.

Tina's mouth dropped open and her eyes bugged as her gaze came to rest on those clasped hands. It had been many years since Nev had held *Tina's* hand the way he was holding hers.

And then he leant forward and kissed her.

A lump rose in Tina's throat and a heavy weight settled on her chest. Tears prickled and, terrified that she might start crying in the middle of Picklewick's high street, Tina forced her numb legs to move.Dragging Daphne along with her, she hurried away, swiftly leaving the café behind.

Nev had found someone else. Her husband had moved on. No wonder Ryan had mentioned the D word. His father must have put him up to it, or at least planted the idea in his head so Ryan would mention it to her.

Oh God, Nev truly *did* want a divorce. He didn't love her anymore and she couldn't blame him.

The only person to blame was *herself*.

CHAPTER TEN

PEANUT HATES ME, Nev thought sadly, as he watched the dog pace up and down the hall for the umpteenth time. Every so often the terrier would whine and scratch at the front door, scrabbling at it until Nev was forced to scold him, whereupon Peanut would resume his pacing.

The dog had seemed happy enough in the café, content to lie under the table with Sheila's dog, Monty, and eat his biscuit while the humans chatted. Sheila was a lovely woman, Nev thought; she'd even suggested that he go for a meal at her house with her and her partner.

But Peanut's good behaviour hadn't lasted. He'd played up all the way home, dancing around on the end of his lead, yanking and pulling on it until Nev had no option but to carry him. And ever since they'd arrived home, the dog had been trying to leave. Nev felt a complete failure as a dog owner. He must clearly be doing something very wrong, but he didn't know what, and repeated internet searches didn't help, providing little in the way of useful information.

The only sensible suggestion was to book an appointment with a vet in case there was something physically wrong. To Nev, it looked as though Peanut was in distress, but he didn't appear to be in pain – if that made any sense. Nev had repeatedly checked him over, running his hands along the dog's body and down his legs, alert to any sign of discomfort. He'd manipulated his joints, felt for lumps, and gently squeezed him all over, but there'd been no indication that Nev's ministrations had been uncomfortable. In fact, Peanut had appeared to enjoy the attention, but the second Nev stopped, Peanut resumed pacing.

Nev was at a loss. The dog was eating and drinking normally, and the opposite end functions were working fine, as evidenced by a cocked leg on the marigolds and a "present" left on the lawn. But it was better to be safe than sorry, so a trip to the vet would hopefully rule out any physical problems, and the vet might even have an explanation for Peanut's behaviour.

So, with an appointment booked for later that day, all Nev could do now was try to soothe his pooch with love and cuddles, and pray there was nothing wrong with the dog who'd wormed his way into Nev's broken heart.

TINA WANTED TO CRY. In fact, that's precisely what she did for the remainder of the afternoon. All she seemed to have done today was weep, and she had no one to blame but herself. She'd had a good man, a good marriage, and a good life – and she'd thrown it all away.

How could she have been so stupid? How could she have been so thoughtless? She had no doubt that she'd hurt Nev badly, so no wonder he'd sought solace in another woman's arms. He'd clearly moved on, and Tina had to accept it. It hadn't been easy seeing him with someone else. She still thought of him as *her* Nev and, let's face it, she hadn't stopped loving *him* – she'd stopped loving what he'd *become*. What *they'd* become: stuck in a rut, set in their ways, and just going through the motions.

She'd so desperately wanted more, but "more" hadn't lived up to her expectations. "More" wasn't much fun now that she was alone. She'd wanted more with *Nev*, not on her own. And now there was no way back to him. He'd moved on. Just like he'd thought she'd done.

Tina couldn't bring herself to disrupt his life again. She couldn't go crawling back begging his forgiveness after what she'd witnessed today. It wouldn't be fair on him, not now that he'd begun to make a new life without her. He'd looked *happy*. That's what hurt the most. Not that she wanted him to be *un*happy, but she just wished he hadn't found someone else quite so quickly.

God, that made her sound such a selfish cow. Like *she* hadn't wanted him, yet she hadn't wanted him to want anyone else. Talk about dog-in-the-manger syndrome.

Tina didn't like herself very much right now. She wouldn't be surprised if Nev didn't like her, either. And their friends clearly weren't that enamoured with her and who could blame them? They were clearly taking Nev's side in all this, and if she were in their shoes, that's what she would do, too.

Tina felt brimful of misery, a dark cloud of despair gathering over her head. She'd made an absolute pig's ear of her life and she had no idea how she could make things better.

Sensing her distress, Daphne, who was curled next to her on the sofa, cuddled in closer, her long muzzle resting on Tina's lap. The dog whined as though in sympathy, and Tina miserably stroked the animal's ears.

'No wonder you're so sad, Daphne,' she told the dog. 'You must be picking it up from me. I'm sorry; you don't deserve to have such a miserable owner.'

Tina just wanted all this to have not happened, to wind the clock back, but that was impossible. All she could do was try to make the best of what she had now, to make a life for herself without the man she was still in love with. She might not love him with the same urgent desperation of those heady early days, but it was a deeper, steadier love that had seeped into her very bones and had become a part of her.

She must have been mad to throw it away. She'd always understood she hadn't stopped loving him, but she'd been under the stupid impression that she loved life more. But how could she, when she'd got her priorities all wrong? One thing was certain: she was paying the price for her stupidity.

It occurred to her that if she couldn't have Nev, she didn't want to remain in Picklewick. It simply wasn't home any longer. What had she been thinking, moving into a cottage in the same village? She should have at least gone to Thornbury, where she could have had a semblance of building a new life. But, oh no, she'd tried to start her new life in the very village where she'd ended her old one. How was that supposed to have worked? She really hadn't thought it through, had she? She hadn't thought at all...

There was only one thing for it: she'd have to move. She couldn't remain in the village with the risk of running into Nev and his new lady friend. She had a couple of months left on the lease of this cottage, enough time to find somewhere else, possibly in Thornbury or maybe even further afield. It would be good for Nev to have some distance too, because he must have been on tenterhooks wondering if she was going to appear round the corner, or bump into her in a shop. It must have been so hard for him.

How could she have done that to him? How could she have done it to *them?*

Feeling sorry for herself, she had another little cry, Daphne whining softly by her side, and when she'd calmed again, she thought this might be a good time to revisit the camper van idea. It would mean selling the house, of course, in order to be able to afford it, and she supposed she should also start divorce proceedings because despite Nev being all cosied up to a woman in the café earlier, he seemed to be in no hurry to formally end their marriage. As usual, it would be up to her. Nev had always left the admin to her, whether it be paying the council tax or getting a quote for car insurance, and this was probably no different. Knowing him, he was undoubtedly hoping it would just magically happen without him having to do anything, and this way it would. All he'd have to do was sign on the dotted line – unless he wanted to contest it. She hoped he didn't. They needed to draw a line under their marriage. There was no point in dragging it out for an extra few thousand pounds.

With a deep sigh, Tina realised she was getting ahead of herself. She hadn't even appointed a solicitor yet and she was already anticipating problems which might never occur.

She typed in *"solicitors near me"* on her phone and it wasn't a surprise to see that there were none in Picklewick itself, and that she'd have to travel to Thornbury.

Choosing one at random, she reached for a notepad but as she finished jotting down the number, the doorbell rang and she clambered to her feet and went to answer it, Daphne padding at her side.

Squinting through the spyhole, Tina saw her youngest son on the pavement. 'Hello, lovely, to what do I owe the pleasure?' she asked, gesturing for him to go inside. Daphne gave him a cautious sniff, then backed away to let him in.

'I just thought I'd call and see how you are.'

'I'm fine.'

'You don't look it. Are you sure?'

'A bit preoccupied, that's all.'

'What with?' Ryan put out his hand and stroked the top of Daphne's head. The dog gazed up at him with large liquid eyes.

Tina didn't want to tell Ryan that she'd spotted his father kissing another woman. First, it would make it even more real; second, he might ask questions she didn't have the answers to; and third, he might know all about it – which would be far worse.

'This little soul,' she said instead and smiled down at the dog. Daphne padded off to her bed and slumped onto it with a loud sigh.

'She's not very lively, is she?' Ryan observed.

'No, I must admit, she's rather on the quiet side. I'm hoping it's just her nature but she does seem rather subdued. Jakob at The Forever Home on Muddypuddle Lane where I got her from, said it might take a while for her to settle in but I'm getting a bit worried.'

'Do you think you could ask his advice?'

'That's a good idea,' Tina agreed. 'Maybe I'll pop up tomorrow and see if I can pick his brains. Tea?' She walked over to the kettle and filled it, then flicked the switch and retrieved a couple of mugs from the cupboard.

When she glanced back at her son, she realised he was staring at the notepad she'd left on the table, where the words "Cornice, Cornice and Motts" were clearly visible. It didn't take a genius to realise that Cornice et al. were most likely a firm of solicitors.

Ryan's expression was questioning. 'You've appointed a solicitor?'

'Not yet. I'm going to, though.'

There was silence for a moment, then he said, 'You're definitely going through with it?'

'It's for the best.'

He looked sceptical, then resigned. 'What happens now?'

She sighed deeply. 'Now we decide who gets what and how much of it.'

'Brutal.'

'Divorces can be, but I'm sure your dad and I can be grown up about it.'

'What will happen to him?'

'What do you mean?'

'Will he be able to afford to give you half the house?'

'I doubt it. It will have to be sold.'

'That's harsh.'

'I know. I feel bad, but that's the way it is. Don't say anything to Dad yet. I want to tell him myself.'

Ryan shook his head, his mouth a thin line. 'I won't say anything, but please don't let a letter from your solicitor be the first he hears of it.'

Tina was aghast. How could her son think such a thing?

Oh, yes… Because she'd walked out on his father. She wanted to protest that she wasn't that cruel, but in Ryan's eyes, she probably was. 'I'll speak to him soon, I promise. Okay?'

'Okay. For what it's worth, I think you're doing the right thing.'

'You *do?*'

'He'll be able to move on. Find someone else.' He gave her a meaningful look and Tina's already bruised heart took another blow as she suspected Ryan knew his father had *already* moved on.

Not wanting to discuss it (she was scared she might cry again), all she said was, 'I hope he will.'

She hoped Nev would be happy with his new woman – he certainly deserved to be. But even as she thought it, Tina had an awful suspicion that *she* wouldn't be happy again because, too late, she'd realised just how much she loved her husband and just how much she'd thrown away.

PEANUT KNEW WHAT kind of establishment it was as soon as Nev put his hand on the door of the veterinary practice and pushed it open. The dog's whole demeanour changed: his ears flattened, his tail drooped, and he seemed to sink into the ground.

Giving Nev an accusing look, he slunk into the waiting room and when Nev took a seat, Peanut hid under it. And there he stayed, glaring apprehensively from behind Nev's legs until a man wearing a blue tunic poked his head out of a door with the words "Exam Room 1" on it and called, 'Peanut Clancy?'

Nev got to his feet. Peanut, unsurprisingly, hung back, so Nev picked him up.

'Hi, I'm Huw, one of the vets. I recognise this little fella – isn't he a rescue from The Forever Home?'

'He is.'

'I thought so. Hello, Peanut.' He stroked the dog's neck. Peanut hung his head and began to tremble. The vet looked at Nev. 'What seems to be the problem?'

'I think he's unhappy.'

'Oh?' Huw's eyebrows rose. 'Why do you say that?'

'I've had him for a few weeks now and he hasn't settled. He barks most of the time, and yesterday he chewed through his lead while we were at the park and ran off. I want to rule out anything physical before I move on to the obvious.'

'Which is?'

'That he doesn't want to live with me.'

'Very sensible to check there aren't any physical issues, but I highly doubt it's the case that he doesn't want to live with you.' The vet looked into the dog's eyes, then checked his gums and teeth. 'Remind me, what's his history?'

'He was a stray.'

'Ah, yes, I remember. He was in fairly good condition when he was brought in, I recall; no fleas, no skin issues, well nourished. He was used to being handled and didn't complain when I gave him his vaccinations and clipped his nails.' He checked Peanut's ears, then listened to his heart and lungs. 'If you hold him, I'll take his temperature.'

Peanut whined, as though he understood what was about to happen, and when it was over he shot Nev a reproachful look. Nev smiled apologetically, but Peanut turned his head away in disgust.

Huw said, 'I can't see anything obvious. Is he eating normally? Drinking okay?'

'Yes to both.'

'What about the other end?'

'Regular as clockwork, straight after breakfast.'

'Have you noticed whether he's limping?'

'He's not limping.'

Huw stood back, eyeing Peanut critically. 'Dogs are very good at hiding pain, but from what I can see, nothing appears to be troubling him. In fact, I'd say he's a perfectly healthy little dog.'

'That's a relief. So what do you think it is?'

'Has he been left alone much?'

'Just the once, and that was for less than half an hour.'

'What about exercise?'

'I take him out twice a day and we do laps of the park, but I'm worried about that now. I mean, he's got a new lead, one he can't chew through, but...' Nev ground to a halt.

The vet said, 'I'm sorry not to be of more help, but it sounds more of a behavioural issue than a physical one. I can give you the names of a couple of people who might be able to shed some light on it, if you want. Failing that, they could at least give you some coping strategies. But before you go down that route, you may want to give Peanut a little more time to settle in. Make sure you're being consistent and if you can stick to a routine, such as set times for meals and walks, that might help. You mention you're worried about him running off? Have you tried the secure dog walking field at The Forever Home? It's called Freedom Field and can be rented by the hour. It would give you peace of mind knowing that he can't escape and it might help the pair of you to build a bond. It should also wear him out.'

Nev thought about it. The suggestion was a good one. At this point, he was prepared to try anything to help Peanut, a sentiment which was reinforced when Nev lifted the dog off the examination table and held him close, and Peanut buried his nose in Nev's neck and gave him a swift lick, snuggling in as hard as he could.

Nev realised it was probably relief on Peanut's part, but he decided to take it as a sign that the dog did love him after all.

It was the only light in what was for Nev, a rather dark tunnel.

CHAPTER ELEVEN

'SHE'S DOING FINE, you said?' Jacob was speaking to Tina but his attention was on Daphne. The hound was standing in the meet-and-greet pen, in her usual tail-down stance.

Tina had walked her up to The Forever Home, hoping the exercise would do them both good, and anyway it took longer to walk than to drive, which meant she didn't have to think about phoning the solicitor just yet. She would do it this afternoon. Depending on what Jacob said, of course.

The dog had been bouncy enough when they'd left the house. Going for a walk certainly appeared to be one of her favourite things to do, and although Tina could understand why dogs liked to go for walks, in the back of her mind she was wondering whether Daphne's enthusiasm was because she didn't like being cooped up in the house with Tina. Anyway, Daphne had remained bright and alert right up to the point where they'd arrived at The Forever Home. But after the initial interest consisting of pricked ears and lots of sniffing, scenting the air with her nose, she seemed to have lost her spark again. Tina just couldn't work her out.

And then suddenly she realised what the dog might be feeling. Today, at least.

'Oh Lord, I should never have brought her here,' Tina lamented. 'She was fine on the way up, but now she's here, she's gone all sad again. I bet she thinks I'm bringing her back.' She knelt on the ground and put her arms around the dog's neck. 'I'm not leaving you, sweetheart,' she promised.

'We've just come to say hello to Uncle Jacob.'

Jacob snorted. 'Uncle?'

'Honorary uncle,' Tina amended. 'The poor thing must be wondering what's going on.'

Jacob gazed critically at the dog. 'She looks healthy enough to me,' he said. 'I'm no vet, but physically there doesn't seem to be anything wrong with her.'

'So you think it's more of a mental issue?'

'Possibly. Though I'm at a loss to know what might be causing it. When she was here, I assumed she was withdrawn because she was finding it difficult to settle into kennel life. I mean, she wasn't totally shut down like some of the dogs we get, but she was certainly not happy being here. She did a lot of pacing around and whining, and every so often she'd howl, which set the other dogs off. It used to drive one little terrier absolutely nuts.' He sighed. 'I'm sorry to say, but the only thing I can think of is that she's pining for her previous owner. Unfortunately there's not a lot we can do about that, but I definitely believe she's bonded with you, so please don't think she hasn't. I know I've said it before, but I'll say it again: it might take her a while.'

Tina got to her feet, one hand resting on the dog's neck. Daphne nudged her with her nose, then whined and took a few paces towards the door.

'I think she's telling you she wants to leave,' Jacob laughed. 'Before you go, why don't you grab a ball or two and take her into our secure field? We usually charge to rent it out, but no one's there right now and I think it would do her good to have a run around. You said you haven't let her off the lead yet, so this would be the perfect opportunity to find out if she'll come back when she's called.'

Tina thanked him, feeling somewhat reassured. She dearly wished she knew what had happened to the dog before she'd adopted her, what her previous life had been like and how she'd been treated.

Oh, I wish you could talk, Tina lamented as she said to Daphne, 'Let's go have some fun.'

She had a feeling that fun had been sadly lacking in the dog's life lately, because living with Tina hadn't been a barrel of laughs, even though she'd given the dog plenty of love and attention, and fed her and walked her; but she hadn't really played with her, had she?

That'll be rectified today, Tina vowed, heading towards the field.

Jacob had given her the combination and she keyed it in, the gate clicking open.

The enclosure was bigger than she expected, a large open space with a couple of benches dotted around, a few trees on the perimeter acting as doggy message boards, and on the far end an agility course had been set up. There was plenty of room to run around, play tug, and fetch.

When Tina unclipped Daphne's harness she stood there uncertainly, staring up at her mistress, seeking reassurance. 'It's alright,' Tina told her. 'Go ahead and have a good sniff. I know you're dying to.'

Daphne didn't need telling twice. With a little wag of the tail she was off, nose down as she worked away around the field, sniffing enthusiastically. But before long, the dog was back, and without Tina having to call her – which was encouraging.

She took the borrowed ball out of her pocket and waved it in the air. 'Look what I've got,' she sang. Daphne followed it with her eyes and then sat on her haunches. 'Do you want to play?'

Daphne leapt to her feet and danced backward a couple of strides, which Tina assumed meant that she did, so pulling her arm back, she threw the ball as far as she could. The second it left her hand, Daphne was off in great leaping bounds.

Gosh, she's fast, Tina thought in awe.

The dog caught the ball as it bounced, leaping into the air and landing lightly on her paws. With it in her mouth, she returned to Tina, her tail waving, wearing a pleased expression. As soon as she reached Tina, she dropped the ball and sat again.

'So *this* is what you like doing?' Tina mused, noting the dog's perkier expression and the light in her eyes.

Picking up the ball, she threw it again. And again. And again.

Tina quickly lost track of the time, too engrossed in the dog's obvious enjoyment, but eventually her arm began to ache, and her throws were becoming more and more pathetic. Daphne was panting as well, although the greyhound showed no signs of slowing down.

'Tell you what, I'll book another few sessions,' Tina said to her, 'but next time I'll be better prepared.' She'd seen some of those long plastic ball thrower things in the pet shop, so on the way home she'd invest in one. Plus a few more balls.

'I think that's enough for today,' she said, clipping the lead back on Daphne's harness and walking her through the gate. 'Let's go get you a drink of water, and I might as well book you in while I'm here.' So with that in mind, she headed towards reception.

Only time would tell whether Daphne's demeanour would improve, but Tina vowed to give it her best shot.

And as soon as she was home, she would set the wheels in motion for divorce proceedings, then she'd have to steal herself to go tell Nev what was about to happen. She wasn't looking forward to it, but she owed him that.

PEANUT'S BEHAVIOUR was good for the walk up to The Forever Home on Muddypuddle Lane this morning. At least it was when they'd set out. By the time they reached the other end of the village, he was starting to get a little manic, either pulling on his lead or stopping frequently to sniff and lift his leg. Nev was fully aware that all dogs did this – not cock their legs, obviously, because female dogs didn't do that kind of thing – but Peanut seemed to be stopping every few seconds. Nev was astounded at how much liquid could come out of such a small dog.

By the time they were through the kissing gate and onto the field, Peanut was practically beside himself. Several times when he stopped to sniff at a clump of grass, Nev had the devil's job dragging him away. Goodness knows what had been in this field previously, but whatever it was had got Peanut all worked up. Rabbits perhaps, maybe a fox, or badgers even? Something was proving irresistible and Nev had to practically haul him up the path.

Hopefully all this excitement, together with being off the lead in the secure field, might wear the little tyke out. He clearly had bags of energy, and Nev worried he wasn't getting enough exercise but he was praying he'd found the perfect remedy. It would be so much easier if Nev could let him off the lead in the park and throw a ball there, but after the lead-chewing incident, he didn't trust the dog one little bit. He didn't actually trust Peanut to come back when he was called in the Freedom Field, so Nev had armed himself with some little treats. He'd give one to the dog before he let him off, so Peanut knew what his owner had about his person, and hopefully whenever Nev showed him the little tub of treats, Peanut would come straight back.

Nev had also worried that by bringing Peanut to The Forever Home, the dog might assume he was being abandoned, but Nev had no need to be concerned because Peanut's excitement actually grew the nearer they got to the enclosed field; it was as though he knew where he was going and what was about to happen. Perhaps he did, Nev mused, remembering how Peanut had watched him stuff a couple of balls into his pocket. Perhaps that's what all this excess excitement was about – Peanut may have been used to playing fetch and he couldn't wait to do it again. He certainly liked playing ball indoors, so it was reasonable to assume he'd enjoy playing ball outside.

Nev took out his phone to remind himself of the pin number for the keypad and he was just about to input it when Peanut went ballistic. There was no other way to describe the dog's frantic barking, lunging, and bouncing around.

'Okay, okay, calm down,' Nev told him. 'If you stop being an idiot for a second, I'll be able to get this gate open.'

The dog was having none of it. But the really odd thing was, he wasn't trying to get *through* the gate and *into* the field – he was trying to get *away* from it.

What an earth was up with him?

Peanut's barking had reached fever pitch by now, and he was practically shrieking. Anyone would think he was being beaten or something. Embarrassed, even though there was no one around, Nev tried to shush him, crouching down and pulling the dog closer in an attempt to soothe him.

It made no difference. If anything, it made Peanut worse. The barking turned into howling, a sound Nev hadn't heard him make before.

Nev was at a complete loss to know what to do. Should he take him home? Or maybe if he waited a minute, Peanut might calm down?

'What's going on?' a voice called, and Nev looked up to see Jacob and the woman from reception hurrying towards him.

'I don't know what's got into him.' Nev had to shout to make himself heard. 'I booked the Freedom Field and was about to key in the entry code and he went berserk. Something's upset him, but I don't know what.'

Jacob dropped to his knees. 'Is he injured, do you think?'

'If he is, I don't see how!' Nev cried. 'He was absolutely fine, and then this happened. Why is he howling like that?' he demanded helplessly.

'Does he do this at home?' Jacob asked, running his hands over the dog's body. Peanut totally ignored him and carried on with his mournful howling.

'Never. It's the first time I've heard him make this kind of noise.'

Jacob said, 'He used to do it a lot when he was here. I wonder if being back has set him off?'

Maisie, the girl from reception, asked, 'Do you need me to call the vet, Jacob?'

Nev hastened to say, 'I took him to the vet yesterday and he was given a clean bill of health, so unless something's happened in the last five minutes, and I can't see that it has, there'd be no point.'

Jacob nodded his agreement. 'I don't think that's necessary, Maisie. Let's see if we can get him to calm down.'

But Peanut *didn't* calm down; in fact, he got worse as another dog's voice joined in the chorus. The terrier immediately ceased howling and began barking, frantic desperate yips and yelps as he tried to wriggle out of his harness.

Answering barks came from behind Jacob, and when Nev peered past him, his mouth dropped open as he saw Tina being dragged across the gravelled area by a rather large greyhound.

Jacob turned to look. 'Tina? Why is Daphne—?' That was as far as he got, as Daphne pulled Tina over.

Tina was forced to let go of the leash and Daphne covered the last few feet in a couple of bounds, knocking both Maisie and Jacob out of the way and sending Nev sprawling in her haste to get to Peanut.

Peanut's barking turned to whimpers and Nev was terrified the greyhound was attacking his little terrier. Scrambling to his feet, he made to intercede and try to drag the other dog off Peanut, but stopped.

Peanut was lying on his back, his little paws in the air, his tail wagging like billy-oh, and Tina's dog was joyfully licking his face. Both dogs appeared to be delighted to see each other.

'Well I never,' Jacob said, his hands on his hips as Maisie hurried forward to help Tina to her feet.

Tina brushed dirt from the knees of her jeans, her expression one of amazement. 'Look at her!' she cried.

Nev looked, but he wasn't sure what he was supposed to be looking at until Tina continued, 'I've never seen Daphne look so happy.'

The greyhound certainly looked quite pleased with herself; *very* pleased, in fact. She was grinning and her eyes sparkled. She kept booping Peanut with her nose, and every now and again she gave him a swift lick on his nose or his ears.

And as for Peanut, he just lay there, doing a sploot, with his back legs stuck out behind him and his tummy flat on the ground. He was the epitome of a relaxed dog, and Nev couldn't believe his eyes.

Jacob scratched his chin and gazed at the dogs with narrowed eyes. 'I get the feeling these two know each other,' he said thoughtfully. 'Wait here. I need to check on something. I won't be long.'

Nev stared after him for a second, then his gaze flicked to Tina. She wasn't looking at him though; her attention was fixed on the dogs and her expression was one of bewilderment.

Nev felt equally bemused. Aside from when the dog was asleep, this was the most relaxed Peanut had been.

'I don't get it,' he said.

Tina shot him a look. 'Neither do I. Daphne is usually so quiet and withdrawn.'

Nev snorted. 'Wish I could say the same about Peanut,' he grumbled. 'That dog is like a kid after eating too many E-numbers. He's always on the go, always shouting about something. But look at him now.'

True to his word, Jacob was back in a jiffy. He was shaking his head.

'What is it?' Nev demanded.

Jacob pulled a face. 'I should have realised – and I would have if they had been brought in on the same day. But they arrived three days apart.'

'What difference does that make?' Tina asked, her eyes troubled.

'They were picked up in roughly the same place. We get a number of strays brought in, but it's unusual to have two brought in within a space of a couple of days, both found in the same place. I should have seen it.' He was shaking his head again.

'Seen *what?*' Nev wanted to know.

'Look at them.' Jakob's gaze was fixed on the animals at his feet. 'There are a bonded pair. I can't believe I missed it.'

'What do you mean, *a bonded pair*?' Tina asked.

'A bonded pair are two animals who have formed a strong attachment to each other. Daphne and Peanut have almost undoubtedly come from the same home. It explains a lot.'

'Is that why Daphne's been so sad? Because she was missing her friend?'

'Is that why Peanut has been so restless?' Nev asked. 'Has he been searching for her all this time?' He sank to the ground, kneeling beside the dogs, and stroked Peanut's head.

Peanut glanced up at him happily

Nev pulled a face. 'No wonder he's been getting excited when he's on a walk. I think he must be able to smell your dog,' he said to his wife.

Jacob said, 'It's my fault. I should have guessed there was something up. His barking used to set the other dogs off, so I didn't think anything of it when Daphne howled, but in hindsight they were obviously calling to each other. The problem was, they were housed in separate kennel blocks and they would have been exercised at different times, so they never actually had a chance to meet. Instead, all they could do was smell where the other one had been and try to keep in touch by barking and howling. If I'd realised, I'd have tried my utmost to make sure they were rehomed together. I feel awful,' he finished.

No one said anything for a moment. The four humans stared at the two dogs, who were perfectly content now they were reunited.

But thoughts whirled through Nev's head like a tornado across Kansas. Peanut and Daphne were a bonded pair, which meant they needed to be together. The problem was, Peanut was his and Daphne belonged to Tina. One of them would have to give up their dog for the benefit of both pooches...

The question Nev was asking himself was, would it be *him* who would do the giving up – or would it be *Tina?*

CHAPTER TWELVE

TINA WAS ASTOUNDED, disbelief flowing through her. *Of all the gin joints in all the towns in all the world... I couldn't make this up,* she thought. Who would believe that she and Nev could separately decide to adopt a dog at roughly the same time, and that those dogs would be a bonded bloody pair?! Daphne couldn't have been bonded to a stranger's dog, could she? Oh, no, it had to be *Nev's.*

A bubble of hysterical laughter rose in her chest and Tina gulped it down, fearing the hysteria might turn to tears. Not only did she have Nev's newfound romance to deal with, but she now had this.

She caught him looking at her and dropped her gaze. There was no way she wanted him to see how she was feeling and she shakily pressed a hand to her mouth, her palm still stinging from the contact with the gravel when Daphne had pulled her over.

'What are we going to do?' Nev asked solemnly.

She looked up. 'What do you mean?'

Jakob shuffled his feet and gave an awkward smile that was more a twist of the mouth than a proper smile.

What was—? *Oh...*

Several things occurred to her simultaneously: Daphne's obvious happiness at finding Peanut again; Peanut's calmer demeanour; Jakob saying that they should have been rehomed together.

As the realisation sank in, Tina began to shake her head. 'No, definitely not,' she stated flatly. 'I'm not giving Daphne up. I *can't.*' The greyhound was ensconced firmly in her heart, and Tina felt sick at the thought of losing her.

There was only one thing for it.

She turned to Jakob. 'If you believe that the best thing for Daphne and Peanut is for them to be together, I'll simply have to adopt Peanut.'

Nev let out an incredulous snort. 'You *will not!*' he cried. 'I won't let you. *I'll* take *Daphne!*'

'Over my dead body!'

'Well, *you're* not having *Peanut.*' Nev repeated, his eyes dark with hurt. 'Haven't you done enough? I can't believe you'd take the *one thing*—' He broke off abruptly, wiping the back of his hand across his mouth.

Tina was floored; and embarrassed too. Wordlessly she picked up Daphne's lead and wrapped it around her fist, shooting Nev a disbelieving look that he could say such a thing at a time like this.

Nev glared back with his *I don't like sprouts* face. The familiarity of it twisted her stomach, and her chin began to wobble. Determined not to cry, she tried to walk away, but Daphne didn't move.

'Daphne, come on,' she urged.

The greyhound refused to budge. She dug her paws in and hunched her back, resisting the pull of the lead.

Peanut scrambled to his feet and whined uneasily.

Although Jakob didn't say anything, he was watching the proceedings carefully. He clearly knew when to butt out and since Daphne was legally Tina's, there wasn't anything he could do. Tina assumed Nev was in the same position, so Jakob didn't have a leg to stand on: he couldn't force either owner to give up their dog.

'*Daphne, come on,*' Tina repeated through gritted teeth, and she tugged harder.

'Oh, for goodness' sake!' Nev muttered. Without warning, he scooped his terrier up and stalked off.

The action took Peanut by surprise and he didn't immediately protest, but after a couple of steps he did, and it was ear-shattering and heartbreaking. The dog yelped and howled as Nev carted him off at a brisk walk.

As soon as Daphne realised what was happening, her resistance magically disappeared and she lunged after Nev and Peanut. Tina's firm grip on the lead brought the dog up short, and she scrabbled for purchase on the gravel, using her weight to try to pull her mistress. Leaning back, Tina acted as a counterbalance, and she was forced to keep that up until Nev was out of sight. Even then, Daphne kept trying to follow them until long after Peanut was out of earshot. Tina's earshot, that is – Daphne's hearing was much more acute than a human.

Gradually the greyhound calmed until she stood there despondently, the epitome of misery, her head down, her tail tucked underneath her tummy, all the fight gone out of her.

Tina's eyes filled with tears and she pressed her lips together. She *was not* going to cry. Not yet. She'd do that later in the privacy of her own home after she'd had time to process what had just happened.

Jakob gave her a solemn nod before walking away, and Tina was grateful for the brief hug Maisie gave her before she also left.

Taking a few minutes to compose herself, Tina crouched down to wrap her arms around Daphne's neck.

'It's alright, girl, it's alright,' she crooned. But it wasn't, was it? Not for Tina, and definitely not for Daphne.

As she walked slowly home, Daphne plodding apathetically beside her, Tina knew what she had to do. And it broke her heart.

NEV WAS EXHAUSTED by the time he kicked the front door shut behind him and deposited Peanut on the hall floor. His arms ached from carrying the wriggling, squirming terrier all the way home, his ears rang from the dog's incessant barking, his head ached, and his heart was shredded all over again. He hadn't thought he could hurt any worse than he already did, but he was wrong. His wife had glared at him with such disdain—

Nev gasped out an agonised breath and he put his hand on the wall for support. Now that he was safely home, the adrenalin that had been keeping him going made him feel shaky and nauseous, and he swallowed hard, his heart pounding, the pain in his chest a living, clawing creature. He'd been aware their marriage was over, but he'd known it in his *head*, not his *heart*. There had been a

kernel of hope in the back of his mind that
maybe his wife would realise she'd made
a mistake and come back to him.

But not now. Not after what had taken
place at The Forever Home.

A boop on the ankle brought him out of his
misery enough to see that he hadn't
removed Peanut's harness. He also
realised he'd fallen blessedly silent, thank
god.

Wearily, feeling drained, Nev tended to the
dog, who promptly trotted off into the
kitchen to noisily lap some water. All that
barking and howling must have made him
thirsty, Nev assumed, hoping that a freshly
lubricated throat didn't mean Peanut
would resume barking. Because if so, Nev
didn't think he could stand it. The dog's
distress tore at him, and for all his bluster
earlier, Nev knew he had a decision to

make. He couldn't, in all conscience, keep Peanut apart from Daphne, not when Peanut's little heart was breaking. Nev loved him too much to be that selfish. He'd allow himself one more night with him, then he'd give the dog to Tina.

Following Peanut into the kitchen, Nev filled the kettle. He didn't really want tea, but that's what people did when they didn't know what else to do with themselves – they had a cup of tea. He had a feeling he'd be making lots of cups of tea in the near future.

Nev had no sooner took a mug off the wooden stand next to the microwave, than Peanut began barking and yipping again.

Nev groaned.

Sinking to the floor, he called Peanut to him. The dog came willingly enough, although he continued to grumble as he put his front paws on Nev's knee.

'Please, please stop, Peanut,' he pleaded. 'I promise you'll be with Daphne tomorrow, but can I just have one more night with you so I can say goodbye properly?' He was almost crying now, his eyes stinging, his throat closing up. How could Tina do this to him? *How?* Hadn't she been content with breaking his heart? Did she have to take the one thing that made his life bearable? She really must hate him.

The doorbell ringing broke into his wretched thoughts and he sighed heavily as he went to answer it, assuming it to be a delivery driver with a parcel for one of the neighbours. But when he saw who was standing on his step, he got the shock of his life.

TINA GAZED AROUND the downstairs living space, searching for anything she may have missed. Daphne's dog bed, along with her toys, her food, the balls, a coat and her harnesses were all by the front door, ready.

A lump rose in her throat and she hitched in a breath. This was going to be hard but it had to be done. Daphne was clearly unhappy at being separated from her little mate, and it hurt Tina to see it. The hurt was twofold, because it meant that Tina was no substitute for Peanut and however much she thought she'd bonded with her dog, Daphne clearly hadn't bonded with *her*. And the second part of the hurt was that Tina would be alone once more.

The thought of adopting another dog flitted through her mind and just as quickly flitted back out again. Even though she knew this situation wouldn't arise again, she couldn't face bringing another animal into the house. Not yet. Give it a few months and she might feel differently. Anyway, she'd have enough to keep her occupied with the divorce and deciding what to do next.

Moving away from Picklewick was still on the cards, but the purchase of a camper van probably wasn't. As romantic as travelling the length and breadth of Britain sounded, traipsing around the UK alone without Daphne to keep her company didn't hold the same appeal. Maybe she would try another trip abroad, she mused, before recognising that she didn't want to do that on her own again, either.

Tina left Daphne lying in the middle of the living room with her nose on her paws, while she loaded everything into the car. The dog was showing precisely zero interest in the proceedings, and she looked more depressed and unhappy than Tina had ever seen her. Which reinforced Tina's belief that she was doing the right thing by reuniting Daphne with her little terrier friend.

When Tina showed Daphne the harness, the dog got to her feet with a distinct lack of enthusiasm, and she simply stood there motionless as Tina secured it around her chest.

Getting on the floor, Tina put her arms around the dog and buried her nose in the soft furry neck, inhaling her unique scent.

'You be a good girl for Nev,' she whispered. 'And have the best life. You deserve it. But god, I'm going to miss you so much!' Then she rose, stealing herself, and attached the lead to Daphne's harness one final time.

The dog sat next to her on the passenger seat, gazing serenely through the windscreen, and Tina pushed aside the thought that this was what it could be like if she and Daphne were to go exploring in a camper van: Tina driving, Daphne riding shotgun, the two of them going on an adventure...

The dog sensed something was up because when Tina turned into the drive and pulled into her usual slot next to Nev's car, Daphne turned to her and whined.

'Don't look at me like that,' Tina said, trying not to read human emotion into the greyhound's accusing eyes. 'This is what you want, *remember?* You want to be with Peanut, and this is the only way it's going to happen. I don't *want* to let you go, but it's the best thing for you, not me. I tried doing what I thought was the best thing for me and look how that turned out. I've been selfish enough already; I'm not going to be selfish now. There's nothing I'd like better than to turn around and take you home, but I'm not going to. I'm going to do what's right for *you*.'

Tina got out of the car and walked around to the passenger side, but when she opened the door, Daphne made no move to jump out. Although it broke Tina's heart to see the dog like this, she took comfort in knowing that in a few moments Daphne would be ecstatic once more.

'Out you get,' she urged, and Daphne reluctantly slunk to the ground. But as soon as she was out of the car, she stiffened, her nose twitching.

Tina said, 'Yes, that's right, you can smell Peanut. No doubt he's scent marked every inch of this drive. Okay, let's get this over with before I change my mind.'

She marched up to the door, thinking sadly that only a few months ago this house had been her home, yet now she was about to ring the bell like a stranger.

Taking a deep breath, she lifted her hand but before she could press the bell, the door opened, making her jump.

'Nev—' she began, then stopped abruptly.

Because it wasn't *Nev* who'd opened the door. It was his new woman.

And Tina felt like bawling.

CHAPTER THIRTEEN

TINA WAS LOST FOR WORDS.

The woman, however, wasn't. 'Oh, hello,' she said, before glancing down at Daphne, her eyes widening. Then she called over her shoulder, 'Nev, there's someone at the door.'

Before Tina could process the thought that the woman seemed rather at home in the house which Tina still technically owned half of, there was a volley of excited barks and Peanut shot past the woman's legs.

And for the second time that day, Tina fell over as Daphne lunged towards her best friend.

'Ow!' she cried, on her hands and knees, her face almost pressing up against the damned woman's legs. The two dogs were prancing around in a flurry of wide-mouthed smiles, wagging tails, and batting paws as they greeted each other.

'Are you okay?' The woman peered down at her.

'I'm fine,' was Tina's curt reply, as she got stiffly to her feet, wincing as she noticed Nev in the hall.

The woman persisted, 'Are you sure? You went down with a bit of a bang.'

'I said, *I'm fine*,' Tina snapped, slapping at the knees of her jeans with palms that had only just stopped smarting from earlier.

'Okay, then,' her nemesis said doubtfully. 'I'll be on my way, Nev, and let you...' She trailed off, before adding cryptically, 'Good luck.' Then she said to Tina, 'I'm Sheila, by the way. Nice to meet you.'

Tina pressed her lips together; this was a difficult enough situation as it was, without having to play nice with Nev's new squeeze, and she followed Sheila with her eyes as the woman trotted down the drive, rounded the corner and disappeared from view.

When Tina turned back, it was to find Nev watching her, his face devoid of expression. He looked tired as he leant against the doorframe, his arms folded.

Tina gestured to her Nissan. 'Daphne's things are in the car.'

His eyebrows shot up and his gaze bored into her. 'You're letting me have her?' His tone was disbelieving.

She nodded.

'Why?'

The question was blunt, and Tina blinked. 'Because she's miserable and I can't stand seeing her like that.'

Nev straightened up, his arms dropping to his sides as his expression hardened. 'It's still all about *you,* isn't it? It doesn't matter what she wants, *you* can't stand her being miserable, so that's why you're giving her up. If you could tolerate seeing her miserable, would you keep her?'

Tina drew in a sharp breath. 'Excuse me?'

Nev muttered, 'Never mind,' then, 'Do you need a hand?'

She supposed she deserved that. Nev was right – she *had* been selfish. But she wasn't being selfish now. Not prepared to argue, all she said was, 'I can manage.'

She couldn't though, and when she struggled to remove Daphne's oversized squashy bed from the car, he let out a huff of exasperation.

'Out of the way,' he ordered, nudging her aside, and Tina caught a whiff of his familiar cologne along with the scent that was uniquely his, and she faltered.

She wanted to reach out and wrap her arms around him; she wanted to bury herself in the warmth and safety of his embrace; she wanted him to love her the way she still loved him. But none of that was going to happen, so she watched him pile Daphne's stuff into the bed and head for the door instead, and held back the threatened tears.

Peanut trotted after him, Daphne on his tail, and Tina drew in a wobbly, pain-filled breath.

'Bye, Daphne,' she whispered, as the dog entered the house and the front door closed behind her. Tina briefly squeezed her eyes shut as she repeated softly, 'Be a good girl for Nev.'

As she slammed the boot of her hatchback shut, her movements jerky, she ached for Nev so much it was as though a hole had been torn in her heart. And Daphne walking away from her without as much as a backward glance, cut Tina to the quick. The hound had also left a hole – a Daphne-shaped one – and Tina would be lost without her.

As she was about to get into the driver's seat, an unearthly noise filled the air and she hesitated. Was that Daphne making that racket?

The howl came again, rising and falling, sending primal shivers down her spine. Why was the dog howling? She was reunited with Peanut, so she had no reason to cry anymore.

Nev appeared in the doorway, Daphne by his side. He was holding her collar, but when he realised Tina hadn't left yet, he released her.

Daphne was on her in a flash, rearing up on her hind legs, her front paws resting on Tina's shoulders.

Tina staggered, then caught her balance. 'Daphne!' she cried, before the dog prevented her from saying anything further by smothering her face in licky kisses, forcing Tina to turn her head away. Tina's spirits lifted with momentary joy before swiftly plummeting again. This was simply dragging out the inevitable.

Daphne dropped to the ground and Tina passed a shaking hand across her face, unsure whether her cheeks were damp from the dog's tongue or her own tears.

When Nev said, 'I think we've got a new problem,' Tina feared he was right.

Daphne was now pressing her body against Tina's legs and uttering little whimpers. Peanut, unsure what had upset his best friend, pawed at her, his expression worried.

Tina gazed at Nev helplessly. It was clear that the dog didn't want her to go, but what choice did she have? None, not if Daphne wanted to be with Peanut. Unless…?

She met Nev's gaze and realised he'd also arrived at the same conclusion. They used to do that a lot, the two of them often on the same wavelength, able to read each other's thoughts. Until they hadn't.

Nev lifted one shoulder in a resigned half-shrug, 'Do you want to come in? It'll take me a few minutes to get his gear together.'

'Nev, I—'

'Don't.' He held up a hand. 'I wouldn't be able to live with myself if I thought not being with you was making Daphne unhappy.' He took a breath. 'In fact, I was going to call round to see you tomorrow and ask you to take Peanut. He cried all the way home and it broke my heart. So you see, you've done me a favour and saved me a trip,' he added, in an attempt at indifference which didn't fool Tina in the slightest.

Turning abruptly, he disappeared inside, and she hesitated before going after him. Mixed emotions filled her as she entered the house she'd lived in for half her life. Its familiarity had an unreal quality, as though a filter had been overlain on it, and she quickly scanned the hall and then the living room for any sign of Sheila's presence.

There were none that she could see, but that didn't mean diddly squat.

Tina suddenly remembered where she'd seen the woman before. It was in the park and she'd had a small fluffy dog with her.

'I know it's no consolation, but at least you'll still be able to cuddle a dog and take it for walks,' she said in a pathetic attempt to make Nev feel better about the loss of Peanut.

'Huh?' Nev had just bent down to retrieve a bright orange ball, but paused to look at her.

'Sheila's dog,' she clarified, but when his expression changed to confusion, she feared she'd got it wrong. 'She does have a dog, doesn't she? A little Bichon? Or have I got her mixed up with someone else?'

'Yes, she's got a Bichon, but why would I take Monty for a walk?'

'Oh, I assumed—' She stopped.

'Assumed what?'

'It's too soon, of course it is. Sorry,' she gabbled.

'Tina, what *are* you talking about?' He reached for a partially gnawed bone, grimaced, and left it where it lay.

'You and Sheila.'

'Me and *Sheila?*'

'I'm speaking out of turn. Your love life is none of my business. Sorry,' she repeated.

'What love life?' he scoffed bitterly. 'I don't *have* a love life. I thought I had a marriage, once upon a time, but I clearly didn't have that, either.' His brows lowered and he glowered at her.

Tina flinched. 'Nev, I—'

'Whatever it is, I don't want to hear it. You've lied to me enough already.'

What had she lied about, she wondered, and was about to ask (because she couldn't leave it there), when she realised what he'd said. 'You and Sheila *aren't* an item?' she demanded.

'No. Not that it's any of your business. Besides, she's got a partner.'

'What was she doing here?'

'She came to see what was the matter with Peanut. She heard him shrieking as I brought him home. The whole village probably heard,' he said bitterly.

'But I saw you kissing?'

'Huh?! *When? Where?*' he scoffed.

'In the café. I *saw* you.'

His face cleared. 'I was *thanking* her.'

'By *kissing* her?'

Nev's expression closed in again and his face darkened. 'You need to get your eyes checked. For your information – and it's still none of your business – I kissed her on the cheek.'

'Why?'

He gave her a thunderous look and Tina backed off. 'You're right, it isn't any of my business, but I—' She couldn't go on. Now wasn't the time to confess that before she'd seen him with Sheila, she'd decided to tell him how she felt, to admit she'd made a mistake and beg his forgiveness. Nev wasn't in the right frame of mind to hear it right now. Maybe he would be—?

Hang on…

'What do you mean *I lied to you*?' she demanded. 'What am I supposed to have lied about?'

'We're going to do this now, are we?'

Tina pulled her shoulders back. 'Yeah, we are.'

Nev drew himself up to his full height. He was a tall man anyway, but he'd lost weight recently and it made him appear taller.

'Okay, you asked for it,' he growled. 'You told me you were leaving because you wanted *excitement*.' He spat out the word. 'Foreign holidays, posh meals and dancing. Yet I've heard on the grapevine that you're going to buy a bloody camper van. Why didn't you just tell me the truth? That you don't love me anymore. Didn't you think I could handle it?' He shook his head. 'What you did was cruel. I spent weeks hoping you'd change your mind, hoping you'd come back to me – but you were never going to, were you? Because you *don't love me!*' He shouted the last, making her jump.

His words also made her heart leap.

'But I do,' she told him softly.

He blinked. 'You do what?'

'Love you.'

'Bullshit.'

'It's true. I always have. It wasn't *you* I fell out of love with, Nev; it was what we'd become – pensioners waiting to die.'

'Speak for yourself,' he grunted.

'We *were*,' she insisted. 'All you wanted was to play bowls or go for a stroll along the canal, and if we're lucky we might stop off somewhere for a sodding coffee as a treat!'

Oh hell, this wasn't the way she'd hoped the conversation would go. They were arguing again, and that was the last thing she wanted. Telling him he was an old fogey was hardly a declaration of undying love, was it?

Tina took a steadying breath and tried again. 'I still love you, Nev.'

He opened his mouth to speak but she barrelled on. 'Leaving you was the biggest mistake of my life. I'm so, so sorry. Please forgive me. *Please*.'

Nev looked dumbfounded. 'You still love me?'

'That's what I'm trying to tell you.'

'And you want me to forgive you? Do you realise how badly you've hurt me?'

Tina hung her head, tears filling her eyes and spilling over to trickle down her cheeks and plop onto her tee shirt. 'Yes.' Her voice was a whisper.

Nev staggered to the sofa and perched on the arm, putting his face into his hands. His voice muffled, he said, 'I don't know if I can.'

She drew in a shuddering breath. 'I didn't think so, but I had to try. I hoped we could try again.'

He groaned. 'Don't do this to me, Tina; I don't think I could survive it if you left me a second time.'

'I won't. I promise.'

He sighed heavily, took his hands away from his face and looked at her. 'I need to think about it,' he said.

'Of course.' She hadn't expected anything less.

Nev got to his feet. 'I'd better finish getting Peanut's things together.'

The dogs were lying side-by-side on the floor watching them with wary eyes, the humans causing them concern.

'Will you be alright without him?' she asked.

'I'll have to be, since Daphne has made it perfectly clear you're not leaving without her and where she goes, so does Peanut.'

But when Tina tried to load Peanut into her car a short time later, Peanut refused to jump in.

'Let me,' Nev said, moving towards the terrier with the intention of picking him up.

The dog thwarted his plans by darting out of reach. Then Daphne compounded the problem by jumping out of the car again before Tina had a chance to buckle her in, and let out a volley of deep barks to egg her little friend on.

'Bugger!' she muttered. 'These two are going to be the death of me.'

'They've certainly got minds of their own,' Nev said, as Peanut scampered back inside the house. 'Since he's refusing to leave, you'll have to take Daphne home without him.'

Nev was right. 'Come on, girl,' she called, patting the passenger seat encouragingly. 'Time to go home.'

Daphne gave her a disdainful look, parked her bottom on the ground and refused to move.

Exasperated, Tina said to her, 'Okay, you're going to have to tell me what's going on, because I don't have a clue...'

'You do know she isn't going to answer you, right?'

'Don't tell me you don't talk to Peanut like he's human, because I won't believe you. Look, she understood what I said,' Tina added, as the dog walked over to her.

Nev began to say something, but whatever it was, he stopped when Daphne gripped the bottom of Tina's tee shirt with her teeth and began to tug at it, trying to pull her away from the car and towards the house.

Tina stood firm. 'Daphne, no. We can't stay here; we've got to go home.'

Daphne's response was to stretch the hem to near tearing point. Grabbing hold of the material, Tina tried to wrest it from the greyhound's jaws, but Daphne refused to let go.

'Nev, some help would be good,' she pleaded, but all he did was stare at her, then turn on his heel and march towards the house.

When he reached the front door, he called over his shoulder, 'You'd better come in – I think we've got some talking to do.'

Both Tina and Daphne paused and stared at each other, then the dog opened her jaws and released her hold on the tee shirt.

'I don't think this is going to be good,' Tina said to her, 'but thanks for trying.'

Tears came again, and she let them flow as Daphne trotted ahead of her. It was time to face the music and Tina was as sure as she could be that the tune wasn't going to be one she wanted to hear.

CHAPTER FOURTEEN

NEV WAS TREMBLING as he strode into the house, making for the living room once more. Daphne pushed past him with a singular lack of manners and went in search of Peanut. From the ensuing whimpers and squeaks of happiness uttered by both dogs, Nev assumed she'd found him.

At least the dogs were happy, so that was something. He wished it was as easy for him and Tina, but a lot of water had flowed under that particular bridge, and he didn't know if he could forgive her.

He *wanted* to, but could he trust her not to feel stifled and unfulfilled again if he took her back? He'd meant it when he'd told her that he couldn't stand it if she left him again.

'I need a drink,' he said, hearing her enter the room behind him. 'Would you like one?'

'Um, water?'

He glanced in her direction, ignoring the tears tracking down her cheeks. 'I was thinking of something stronger.'

'Oh. I'll have a gin then, please.'

Nev poured two, making them doubles, and added a splash of tonic. He placed her drink on the coffee table, scared to get too close in case he gave in to the urge to sweep her into his arms and carry her upstairs.

Gripping his glass tightly, he downed half his gin in one go. Unfortunately the sudden hit of alcohol to his system didn't have any effect. He still felt shaky. He felt angry, too. And hopeful. The hope was the scariest part.

Taking another, smaller mouthful, he said, 'You weren't happy before. Why do you think you'll be happy if you come back?'

Tina dashed away her tears with the back of her hand, and his heart went out to her. He desperately wanted to comfort her but he resisted.

'Because I now know what unhappiness really is; it's being without *you*,' she said, blinking hard. She was trying not to break down, he realised, and he did some blinking of his own.

She whispered, 'I don't know what else to say. How can I convince you I mean it?'

'I don't know if you can.'

Tina hung her head. He studied the delicate curve of her neck, the upturned nose, the generous mouth, and imagined never seeing those features again. Never holding her again. Never being with her again.

The vision was a hellish one. One that he'd been existing in since she'd walked out.

She said in a strangled voice, 'Do you want a divorce?'

'God, no!' He was adamant about that and had replied without thinking. But if they weren't going to divorce, then what was the point of living separate lives? They were either married, or they weren't. No half measures.

Speaking of half measures... Nev topped up his glass, but Tina shook her head when he offered to refresh hers.

'I've got to drive home.'

No half measures, he told himself again. The decision was a black or white one. Black was a future without his wife in it.

Nev voted for white.

'Not if you don't want to,' he replied. 'This is your home.'

Her damp eyes widened and her lips parted. She drew in a deep breath, letting it out slowly. 'You forgive me?' she whispered.

'I love you,' he replied simply. If it meant being with her, he'd forgive her anything. He'd *do* anything. She was his world, and if travelling the globe would make her happy, he'd take her to the ends of the earth and back again.

TINA LOOKED DEEP into her husband's eyes and saw the love and sincerity in them.

'Thank god,' she breathed, her heart aching with love for this man that she'd hurt so badly, yet who was willing to forgive her and give their marriage another chance.

He held out his hand, and as she slipped her palm into it and he pulled her towards him, she vowed to spend the rest of her life making him happy. And if that meant gentle strolls by the same canal they'd walked along countless times before, then that's what she'd do. That's what *they* would do – the four of them. Two humans, two dogs, and a whole lot of love.

Who needed an exotic foreign holiday, when they had each other?

But there was *one* thing she was hoping to persuade him to try... She wouldn't mention it yet though, because he was kissing her in a way he hadn't kissed her since they were first married and it stole her breath until she couldn't think of anything other than the man she'd vowed to love and cherish for the rest of her days.

TINA LIFTED THE FLUTED glass to her lips, took a sip of chilled tart wine and murmured, 'Ah, this is the life.'

'Isn't it just?' her husband of thirty-five years agreed. It was their wedding anniversary and they were celebrating in style. A style that involved a fantastic view over a valley patchworked with fields in various shades of green, edged with the darker shades of the hedgerows and dotted by stands of trees. In the distance, a church turret was visible.

The peace was profound, with only the occasional bleat of a distant sheep or the trilling call of a skylark to disturb it. Oh, and Peanut's snoring. For such a small dog, he was an incredibly loud sleeper.

He and Daphne were sprawled on a blanket on the grass, exhausted from the long walk they'd been on earlier, undertaken before it became too hot for such exertions. It might be September, but an Indian summer was in full swing and it was unseasonably warm for early autumn. Perfect weather for spending time with Nev's new woman.

She was called Winnie and was small, cute, and as far as Tina was concerned, a brilliant addition to the family. Nev was quite taken with her too, and Tina hadn't even had to talk him into it. When she'd suggested they buy a camper van as a compromise between her yearning to travel and his penchant for the comforting and familiar, he'd agreed to take a look.

'Only a look, mind,' he'd warned. 'We're not going to buy anything today.'

Nev had driven it home four days later, having fallen in love with it and paid a deposit there and then to secure the vehicle.

As a four berth, there was plenty of room, with a bed over the cabin, a small kitchen towards the front, a minuscule shower-cum-loo, and a lounge area to the rear. It had satnav, a solar panel on the roof, and an awning attached to the side, so they could put a table and two folding chairs in its shade if they wanted. Like today.

This was a trial run to iron out the wrinkles before their planned trip to Devon in a couple of weeks. And so far everything was going swimmingly. Tina was having a lovely time. They all were, even though they hadn't technically left Picklewick – the van was parked on the top of the mountain, not far from The Forever Home on Muddypuddle Lane but far enough so as not to be disturbed by the kennels' vocal residents.

It was their second day in the van, and Tina felt as though she'd been on holiday for a week. It was amazing what a change of perspective could do, she thought. In more ways than one!

'What do you fancy doing now?' Nev asked, and she glanced across at her husband.

He looked so relaxed, his legs encased in board shorts, stretched out in front of him, tanned and lean, his head tilted up to the sun, his eyes closed. The beard he'd allowed to grow suited him, and a flush of desire heated her cheeks.

'We could take a nap?' she suggested wickedly.

He opened one eye. 'A nap, huh?'

'Yep.'

'I'm not sleepy.'

'Neither am I.'

'Woman, you're insatiable.'

'Just how you like me.' It was fun flirting with him. She'd found herself doing that a lot lately.

He opened the other eye and stretched languidly, his arms above his head. His tee shirt rose to expose a band of flat stomach, and she ran her tongue over her lips. He'd lost weight and had become more toned since he'd adopted Peanut.

So had she; Daphne had been good for her, too.

Nev's slow smile lit up his face and her heart fluttered with the same excitement she'd felt in the early years of their marriage, before children, busy lives, and the passage of too many years had taken its toll.

But now this was *their* time, to spend together, and Tina intended to make every day count. They'd already made a good start.

Nev got to his feet. Both dogs were instantly alert.

'We're going for a nap,' he told them, and Tina let out a giggle when Peanut stood, turned in a circle and slumped down again with an exaggerated huff, his back to them.

Daphne stayed where she was, but her eyes followed Tina and Nev as they trotted up Winnie's steps and went inside.

Tina knew the dog would remain awake and on guard until her humans reappeared, and gratitude swept over her. Daphne had brought Tina and Nev back together, and she fully intended they stayed that way.

Tina's final thought before Nev took her to bed was *never underestimate the power of a dog*.

There are loads more large print books in the Muddypuddle Lane series. Available at all good book stores, or ask your local library.

About Etti

Etti Summers is the author of wonderfully romantic fiction with happy ever afters guaranteed.

She is also a wife, a mum, a pink gin enthusiast, a veggie grower and a keen reader.

9 781915 940452